Playing Dead

by

Jody E. Lebel

This is a work of fiction. Names, characters, places, and incidents are either the product of the author's imagination or are used fictitiously, and any resemblance to actual persons living or dead, business establishments, events, or locales is entirely coincidental.

Playing Dead

COPYRIGHT © 2012 by Jody E. Lebel

Cover Art by *Kim Mendoza*

The Wild Rose Press
PO Box 708
Adams Basin, NY 14410-0708
Visit us at www.thewildrosepress.com

Publishing History
First Crimson Rose Edition, 2012
Digital ISBN 978-1-61217-107-4
Print ISBN 978-1-61217-106-7

Published in the United States of America

"Detective Graciano. From yesterday?"
He held out his hand but quickly took it back
when Renee ignored it.

She crossed her arms and faced him squarely. "I remember you, Detective. I'm not simple minded."

"Well, you're acting like it."

"I beg your pardon?" she said through clenched teeth.

"I see this kind of thing all the time. That man is a con, and he's taking advantage of you."

"You don't know that," Renee said, dismissing his advice, and him, by turning her back. She struggled to appear cool and in control. Despite being ticked off at his remark about her mental status, the nearness of him made her pulse race, and something was definitely going on with her knees. She handed Eddy the docket sheet and closed her purse with a sharp snap. "Why aren't you out working on Liz's case?" she flung over her shoulder. "Stay out of my business."

"Seeing people get fleeced is my business, Ms. Rose," he said. "I can't stop you from doing this, but if you don't really know Pretty Boy over there, you shouldn't get involved."

Renee barely controlled a shiver when he said her name. *What? Are we in high school now?* She struggled to bring herself under control, then turned and confronted the detective dead on.

"I didn't ask for a lecture. I have a father for that. I'll run my own life." He started to open his mouth, but she held up her hand. "Again, let me remind you it's none of your business." She kept her voice unfriendly but low, aware that they were a source of amusement to the people around them. "Why don't you concentrate on pulling *yourself* together?" She waggled her fingers at his crumpled shirt and hideous tie. "And leave me alone."

Dedication

To Mary Schmidt and Judy Orena,
two good friends
who were there when I needed them.
And to Suzy Suddarth, my inspiration for Liz.

Chapter 1

His Stun Gun

"Dead men don't send e-mails, Liz, particularly men who have been buried for over a year." Renee enveloped her friend in a protective hug and then bent down to pat Liz's dog, Beans, who jumped around her legs in happy little circles.

"I know." Liz sniffed into a coffee-stained napkin. "That's why I called the police. It's so creepy."

Liz pulled Renee in from the sun porch, shut her front door against the muggy South Florida air, and went in search of a tissue. She came out of the bathroom clutching a wad of toilet paper. "It's only been a week since I got Steve's life insurance check."

Renee tossed her purse on the hallway stand and headed toward the open laptop. She peered down at the glowing screen and took a moment to calm herself. Stomach tight with the potential drama about to unfold she worked the mouse and brought the message to life. When her hair fell into her eyes, she twisted it back and secured it with a pen plucked from a mug on Liz's desk. The mug read "Court reporters do it in strokes."

"It can't be him," Renee muttered, hoping for all the world she was right. "I went to this man's funeral."

On a calm morning a little over a year ago,

Steve had taken his boat out for a day of fishing. The vessel had been found empty miles out at sea, engines as cold as the beer in the ice chest. Three months before the wedding, Liz had lost her groom.

"Of course it can't be him," Liz agreed, straightening stacks of transcripts. "Will you look at this place?" she said, casting a critical eye around the room. "The cops will be here any minute now." She swept a hand across her desk and pushed piles of crisp paper steno notes into the top drawer.

"They won't care what your apartment looks like," Renee said over her shoulder. "This is a palace compared to the dumps they usually get called out to."

"Yeah, that's true." Liz hesitated a moment then began stuffing slippers behind a couch cushion and kicking dog toys under the ruffle of the easy chair. Beans hopped up on the sofa, dug behind the cushion, and enthusiastically dragged one soft pink slipper back out.

Renee watched her friend bustle about. It had been a tough year of wondering, waiting, and finally mourning. Liz had lived inside Steve's memory the way a goldfish lives in a bowl, as if that's the only world that existed. When the late-night tearful calls came, Renee had brought over bottles of red wine, cooked lots of comfort food, and gently eased Liz back into life post Steve. Now this. This could be a major setback.

Renee tilted the laptop cover backward to brighten the screen. "Although, they never did find Steve's body." Liz stopped straightening and came over to stand beside her friend, the blue of the screen casting an eerie glow on her face. "How odd that there's no sender's name," Renee muttered, steering away from body talk, sorry she had brought it up. Renee gently tapped the area where that information normally would be found. "I've never seen that spot blank before."

Liz jerked her thumb at the computer. "You know when I first read that it physically hurt." She touched her breastbone and rubbed lightly.

Renee swiveled in the chair and placed a comforting hand on Liz's back. They remained in that position, secure in friendship and united in old wounds, until Liz spoke again.

"When I heard the thudding in my ears," she said quietly, "I realized I might be fainting, so I sat down before I fell down. But once I got my breath back and read it again, I knew. I knew it wasn't Steve." Her voice gained strength and volume. She held her chin up. "He was an English major before he became an engineer, for God's sake. Look at that grammar. Look at that spelling. Whoever is doing this, he sure isn't my Steve. This is some—some crackpot. Or a crackhead maybe."

Liz sniffed loudly but squared her shoulders. "I wish I had a shot of tequila." She looked wistfully toward the kitchen. "I might have some in the cupboard."

"Bad idea. You don't want tequila on your breath when you talk to the cops."

Beans jumped into Renee's lap and the three of them studied the message.

Don't be scared and don't panic. I'm safe now. Don't have much time to write. I need you're help. Will need money. I could be home for Christmas.

Love, Steve.

P.S. Barking dogs can't fly without umbrillas.

"This is pretty lame," Renee said skeptically. "He'll be home for Christmas? That's just a few days away." Renee read it again out loud. "Umbrillas? And what's that barking dogs can't fly stuff?"

"That's a silly little thing Steve and I did." Liz cleared her throat and took a moment before she continued. "It's a line from a movie. He used to sign

3

cards like that." A tear made its way down Liz's cheek. She let it reach her chin before wiping the back of her hand across her face.

"Who else knows about the barking dogs thing?"

Liz shook her head and closed her eyes. "I don't think anyone does." Her voice dropped so soft and low that Renee had to lean closer to hear. "That's what kind of threw me."

Renee studied her best friend's face, searching for signs of how badly Steve's miraculous reappearance, if only in writing, upset her. She had known Liz for over twenty years, since court reporting school. Together they had been through it all; husbands, childbirth, divorce, death, frustration and laughter. Liz's lip trembled, but at the moment she appeared to be holding on.

A loud knock made them jump. Beans erupted in a burst of frenzied barking and promptly ran over to the door and took a protective stance.

"They're here," Liz said. She smoothed back her blonde hair and wiped her hands on her jeans. "I guess I'll let them in," she added, but she didn't move.

"Good plan." Renee waited a moment before putting a hand on Liz's back and gently propelling her forward. Renee scooped up the dog, then stepped back so Liz could unlock the door.

Expecting to see a couple of uniforms from the Jacaranda Police Department, to Renee's surprise two plain-clothes detectives appeared in the doorway.

"I'm Detective Grace Slikowski." The female officer nodded her head to her left, "And this is my partner, Detective Anthony Graciano."

Although not textbook handsome, something about the male detective shot a little bump of adrenaline straight to Renee's libido. Orange Alert. Or in this case, Blue Alert. Oh, no, no. No cops for her. Renee had sworn off law enforcement officers after her disastrous marriage to one had ended four years ago. In her experience, being with a cop was a lot like getting a bikini wax; it starts off hot, quickly turns painful, and you end up crying.

Detective Slikowski was slight and pretty, almost elegant. Eyeing her perfectly swept up and pinned auburn hair, Renee found herself making furtive motions to fix her own hastily twisted-up mop. The detective's matching jacket and skirt were neatly pressed, and when she extended her hand, her nails appeared salon fresh. She entered the house with the air of authority that only cops have, but left behind a cloud of expensive perfume. The woman's cool manner and confidence had a visibly calming effect on Liz. Detective Slikowski followed her to the office area to inspect the laptop.

Detective Graciano was his partner's antithesis. He needed a haircut, and his five o'clock shadow looked spectacular considering it was only two in the afternoon. The hard lines of his face accented his intense green eyes; eyes that would surely make a person talk if they were unlucky enough to be interrogated by him. This was the kind of man that gave everything to the job and had nothing left when he came home. This was the kind of man that could scar a woman for life. This was the kind of man that, in her younger years, Renee would have given a hot tumble.

Unable to control her curiosity, Renee checked out his left hand. No ring. She should have guessed there was no woman in his life by the way he dressed. His crumpled shirt was half tucked into dress pants that must be from the 90's. And that tie? It was horrible.

He seemed happy standing in the doorway. Renee wondered how long she should wait him out, aware of the air conditioning escaping out into the neighborhood. The smell of freshly mown grass wafted in.

"You know, your bell's broken. Might want to get that fixed," he said, never taking his eyes off the notepad he scribbled in. Renee peered around at the offending bell.

"Uh, okay. I'll tell Liz." The man stood in the doorway while the Sunday activities in Liz's neighborhood played out behind him. Kids in neon colored helmets rode their bikes in twos and threes. Mrs. Kelsey across the street was watering her flowers with a bright green hose. Somewhere a lawn mower hummed. Renee stepped aside to give him room to enter. No movement. She swept her free hand toward the interior of the house in a welcoming gesture. Nothing. She waited. Crickets chirped. If this were a cartoon, a tumbleweed would have rolled by.

"You going to come in or what?" she finally asked, deliberately keeping her voice in a friendly mode while trying to prod him off the stoop. She was determined to be nice to law enforcement even if it killed her. He stopped writing in his notepad for a moment and fixed the dog with a baleful glare.

"She's all bark," Renee said, trying to shush the Yorkie, who had taken it down a notch but still yapped away in her arms. The detective stood cemented to the spot. "Her name's Beans." When Renee held the dog up to show off her cute little face, the detective jerked backward.

"She's only seven pounds." Renee said, unable to conceal her amazement that he was afraid of a dog named Beans. "Don't you chase dangerous criminals and stuff?"

"Yeah, but I carry a gun for them. I can't shoot a dog. It wouldn't look good on my record. And the paperwork?" He looked heavenward and rolled his eyes.

His rich, deep voice felt like a caress against her skin. Her lower body stirred. Images of him whispering things to her in bed danced around in her head. Renee blinked rapidly, licked her lips, and blew out a little breath. She needed to pull herself together. There seemed to be some sort of chemical thing going on here. She hadn't been involved with anyone for a long time, and she had no plans to get involved anytime soon.

"Look," he said, "over the years I've been bitten lots of times by cutesy-looking dogs." He looked intently down into her eyes and Renee momentarily forgot what they were talking about. She'd definitely have to watch herself with this guy. Cops made terrible boyfriends and worse husbands. Even crooks had better relationships and fewer divorces than cops. Probably because they had no career pressures to deal with. Unless, of course, you classified breaking and entering as a career.

"Why don't you let me close the door before every bug in town comes in?" Renee said pointedly, mentally and physically pulling herself away from him.

He hesitated.

Renee held the dog up with one hand. Beans' tags jingled and she stopped barking. "Don't worry, I'll protect you from Killer here," she said, drawing her eyebrows together in a deadpan serious expression.

"Very funny," he said, but Renee found it hard to hear with all those warning bells going off in her head. Beans squirmed to get down. "See, she likes you." Renee placed the dog on the floor.

The detective side-stepped into the room just far enough for Renee to close the door. Beans sniffed and wiggled all over the place, trying to get the new visitor's attention.

When Renee turned from locking the door, her

breast brushed against the detective's arm. "Oh, I'm sorry, I..." She let it dangle. She had nothing to be sorry about. She found herself blushing, something else she hadn't done in years.

He grinned down at her, a genuine grin that cancelled out his dark and dangerous look. When the smile reached his dimples, Renee lost her breath. She took a quick step back and tripped over the dog. The detective grabbed for her arm and yanked her toward him to steady her. Her shoe came off as she fell against the length of him, surprised to find his chest more solid than she would have thought under those sloppy clothes. Apparently, he couldn't iron a shirt, but was able to find the gym.

They stood like that for what seemed an eternity. She became aware of his warm fingers on her arm, of the pulse in his neck, of something hard in his pants. Heat swept down her spine and it had nothing to do with the door being open so long. She might have moaned a little.

"Are you happy to see me or is that your stun gun?" Renee whispered, mortified with herself as soon as it came out of her mouth.

He raised his eyebrows. "It's a big one, isn't it?" he said, playing along, clearly teasing her.

"Depends on what you're used to, I guess," Renee shot back, righting herself and pulling away from him.

Renee's heart thudded in her ears. This guy was going to be a challenge. He had to be over six feet tall, because straight on she stared at his mouth, and she was tall. And she was acutely aware of his mouth as he slowly released her. What kind of tough guy had dimples? She fought the urge to touch them. She tried to compose herself and found she didn't know what to do with her hands.

Getting back to business, he flipped open his pad. "Let's start with your name."

"Oh, I'm not the complainant," Renee said, horrified as her hands fluttered of their own accord around her head. She made fists and forced them to her sides. Now it was worse; she was standing ramrod straight. "My friend, Liz Sutton, called you."

"Nevertheless, I'll still need your name." His eyes challenged the color of leaves after a summer rain and were fringed with dark lashes any woman would kill for. He rubbed the pad hard with his pen, making little circles. "Darn thing just ran out of ink," he said, a scowl darkening his face.

Renee reached to the back of her head, pulled out the pen that had been holding her hair in place, and offered it to him. Her hair fell. She shook her head to straighten it, aware that he had begun to stare at her, aware too that she was overdoing the hair-shaking thing because he was staring. She had to get away from this man before she asked him to marry her.

The female detective looked over and let out a *tsk* that could probably be heard down the block. "Stop fooling around and come look at this," she said, one hand on her hip, the other pointing to the screen.

Detective Graciano straightened his obnoxious tie and strode over to her. "I'm not fooling around, I'm conducting an investigation."

"Of her person?"

"She tripped over the dog."

"And fell on *you*?"

"I was there. I don't think I'm supposed to let civilians fall on the floor. Protect and serve. Sound familiar?"

"Fix your shirt. Do you know your bottom button is missing?" She pointed at the e-mail. "You want to give this a shot sometime today?"

Renee listened to the easy exchange between the officers and smiled. Although drastically different, these two appeared to genuinely like each other. Renee slipped on her shoe and joined the group at the desk. Detective Slikowski had been asking Liz questions and had a pad full of notes. Detective Graciano sat in front of the computer and began tapping keys.

"Does he know what he's doing?" Liz asked. "I've got depositions on there."

This was met with a sour look from Graciano.

"He knows his way around a computer," Detective Slikowksi assured Liz. "He won't erase anything."

He typed in commands one after the other, entering them in a rapid-fire style. A few moments of silence followed while he frowned at the screen, then a few more hesitant taps.

"Aha, here it is," Graciano said, raising his fist in a triumphant gesture.

They all peered at the screen. Liz frowned. "That's a coupon for a free pizza."

"I know. I've been searching for this for days. I'll just print this out real quick." He hit a key and the printer buzzed to life.

"Did you check his badge?" Liz asked, looking first at Renee, then to Detective Slikowksi. "He is with you, right?"

"Graciano, you're embarrassing me," the female detective said, but the way she said it made Renee think she wasn't all that upset. "Stop playing around with—"

"Okay, fine," he interrupted. "I sent a query into the system; I was just waiting for the answer." He tapped the screen with a pencil eraser. "Here's the sender's info. Don't shoot the messenger."

Detective Slikowski scrutinized what he pointed to, then wrote a few lines in her pad. She turned to Liz and Renee. "Muffdiver3. Are either of you familiar with him?" Renee shook her head. At the disgusted look on Liz's face, the detective added, "I guess that's a no. Okay, I think we have everything we need for now."

She handed Liz a card. "We'll check out this information, Ms. Sutton. It sounds like someone may be trying to shake you down for the insurance money you were telling me about. Don't respond to this e-mail. In the meantime, if you hear from this guy again, call me." Detective Slikowski slid her pad neatly into her designer purse. "We'll be in touch."

The two detectives made their way to the door.

"Want me to tie up the dog?" Renee asked, careful to keep her expression blank.

"Cute. Very cute," Graciano said.

Yes, you certainly are, Renee thought, then mentally thunked herself on the head.

After the two detectives left, Liz looked over at her friend. "I thought cops were still off limits. What was that all about over by the door?"

"Oh, I don't know," Renee said, irritated with herself. So she had had a hormonal rush. So what? It just proved she wasn't dead.

"Now can I get the tequila?" Liz rummaged in the fridge until she found the margarita mix and a lime. Ducking her head under the counter to pull out the blender, her voice became muffled. "I wonder why we haven't seen those two around the courthouse before. He's kind of hot with that bad-boy look, but he's a fashion disaster."

Renee couldn't disagree. "If that's Jacaranda's finest, maybe we should move." Renee felt glad Liz had stopped crying and seemed back in control. Speaking with the cops appeared to have been therapeutic for her.

"Did you see his tie?" Liz asked, rinsing out the pitcher. "It was pitiful."

Renee nodded and wrinkled her nose in answer. Now that he was handling Liz's case, they would probably see a lot more of him. The low simmer of attraction between them had gotten her juices flowing. There was a certain relief in knowing that they could still flow, and a certain frustration in not knowing what to do about it.

She headed back to the computer. "Did you see where he got that coupon from?"

Chapter 2

Crappy Handwriting

People didn't come back from the dead. Ever, period. She couldn't count Jesus. That had been two thousand years ago, and some people still didn't buy that story. The miracle thing wouldn't work here. Making her sister believe Steve was still alive was going to be a bitch.

"Stealing the laptop was brilliant, huh?" Monica said.

When Richard didn't answer, she frowned and cursed her back luck with men. Why did she always pick losers? Booze and drugs were making him stupid, killing off thousands of brain cells every day. They were practically falling out of his ears. How soon before he forgot how to make a peanut butter and jelly sandwich? She knew she wasn't all that bright, but she liked being smarter than him.

"You heard me?"

"Yeah, yeah. Brilliant."

"It's imperative that this project be successful," she lectured, mimicking her eighth grade English teacher. The grade she almost finished.

"Well, la-de-da," Richard shot back. "Where'd you get them big words? Come over here and put a few in this then, if you so smart."

Monica was impressed with herself. She liked the word imperative. She rolled it around in her head. She knew some big words, unlike her moron boyfriend.

Sprawled in the motel room chair, one leg dangling over the worn arm, she studied him as he labored over the computer. If this plan worked, she could step back into a normal life, get out of this dump, and stop committing suicide one white line at a time.

Richard's fingers moved clumsily around the keyboard, searching for letters, hitting buttons in an uneven beat.

"Why don't these keys look more familiar?" he complained. "I know I took typing in high school. Did they change the board?" He peered down at the panel suspiciously. "They musta' changed it."

"High school?" Monica snorted. "That was twenty years and a hundred thousand cells ago."

Richard's face wrinkled in confusion. "Cells?"

"Never mind."

The room was quiet except for the drone of an ancient AC unit mounted in the window. The cold air hurt her head, but she left the setting on high to keep them awake. Condensation dripped steadily from the bottom corner, soaking the wall, leaving an ugly brown streak. The sharp, moldy odor stuck in the back of her throat, and she cleared it often.

Richard sat, cross legged in the middle of one of the rumpled beds. An unattended cigarette with a long ash rolled off the ashtray next to him and touched his leg. Keeping his eyes on the screen, he reached for it, cursed when he brushed the hot end, and then clamped it between his teeth. He hit a few more keys then backspaced. Delete, delete, delete. Ashes sprinkled over the keyboard. Richard blew them off with a disgusted grunt, then stubbed out the half-finished cigarette with such force it cracked the plastic ashtray.

Monica untangled herself from the chair. She

flopped on the bed and frowned at the short paragraph, willing it to come together.

"Don't crowd me," he complained. "Stop looking over my shoulder."

"It don't look any longer than it was two hours ago. What the hell have you been doing all this time?"

Lack of sleep made her cranky. She looked wistfully over at the top of the scarred dresser, hoping to see some white powder they had missed. No such luck.

"You wanna get some sleep and work on this later?" he said, hope clear in his eyes.

"No, no, no. We gotta keep hittin' her with these. If we give her a break, she might stop and think." Monica fixed him with an imperious stare. "That's psychology, you know."

Richard gave her a dubious look. "What do you know about psychology?"

"More than you," she shot back.

A few minutes passed in silence. "You gonna do this or not?" she asked, her voice dropping into a whine.

Richard jumped off the bed and started pacing around the small room, muttering to himself, trying sentences out loud, gesturing with his hands. He stopped abruptly and scowled down at the blue square. No ideas appeared to be coming. Monica knew he wasn't an idiot. At one time, he had been a successful businessman. His bar, a popular after-work spot for the downtown legal crowd, had netted him friends, the feel of expensive suits, and a pretty wife waiting at home. But that was all pre-cocaine. His pretty wife still waited at home, but now it was for somebody else. Richard doubled up a fist and knocked on his forehead, cursing softly.

"Why don't you take a little break," Monica suggested, trying a new tact. "Clear your mind."

"Yeah, yeah. Maybe that's what I need."

Richard stretched his arms over his head, then jogged in place a few times. The room stank of sour food and days-old sex. He strode over to the front door and flung it open.

"You know you're in your shorts, right?" Monica went over to the window and peered out.

Two women, apparently still woozy from a long night of partying, were walking unsteadily to their car. A snort of laugher drifted over the parking lot.

"Nice legs," one of them threw over her shoulder. "All three of them." The second one squealed in mock horror and pushed her friend forward.

Richard made a face at them and slammed the door.

"I told ya," Monica said, closing the blinds.

"This room is a mess," he complained.

"Yeah, well, this dump don't have no room service." Monica flopped back on her bed and settled in the saggy middle. A hole in the bedspread caught her eye and she began to pull at the threads. Richard collected half eaten boxes of chicken, sticky Chinese food containers, and bent, burnt soda cans. Into the tiny waste basket they went. He picked his shirt off the floor, held it against his body, and carefully smoothed the wrinkles out with his hands. Then he put it on a wooden hanger and hung it in the closet. The only thing in there.

Finding his socks under the dresser, he jammed them into his shoes which he placed on the shelf above the shirt. When he kicked Monica's clothes into a pile against the far wall, she protested by giving him the finger.

His reflection, caught twice in the cracked mirror, stopped him and he turned to study his image. It appeared to disturb him. He moved closer and peered at his face, scowling as he ran a palm roughly over his chin.

"When was the last time you shaved or showered?" Monica said, knowing it had been days. "Don't bother cleaning the room, it's you that stinks."

Richard dismissed her comment with a back wave of his hand. The guy in the mirror had long and unruly blonde hair. She watched him pull the skin down under his eyes and examine his pupils.

"You know what you're looking for?" Monica asked. He had lost a lot of weight and he looked like hell.

"Sex, drugs, and rock and roll," he whispered.

Richard cracked his neck and popped opened a can of warm soda. After a long swallow, he positioned himself in front of the computer. He ran his fingers through his hair, pushing it back out of his eyes. Flexing his wrists dramatically, making Monica roll her eyes, he started typing. After a few moments, he paused, frowned, cursed, hit the delete button. Then a quick tap-tap-tap of keys.

"That sounds like shit," he muttered. He slumped back on the bed, legs on either side of the screen.

"This don't have to be perfect," Monica rolled on her side. Lord knows the last one wasn't. "It just has to knock her shoes off."

Richard reached over to the side table for another cigarette, lit it, and took a deep drag. "That's socks."

"Huh?"

"It has to knock her socks off."

"Whatever. Read what you have so far."

He sat up and propped the computer on his knees.

Will need money to pay the bribe. Its been a nightmare, but it's almost over. Can't wait to see you again.

Love, Steve.

17

P.S. Topless in Massachusits.

"Well, that's crap," Monica whined.

"What did you write, huh? Nothing. Not one damn word. Shut the hell up."

He stared down at the message. "Is this right?" He turned the laptop toward her and pointed to the word "Massachusits."

Monica tried to focus without leaving her bed. "It don't look right."

"Do you know how to fix it?"

"No, but it's an important part, it has to stay. Let me see the letter again."

Richard tossed over a crumpled paper. Monica smoothed the letter they had chosen, then studied it, her face screwed up in concentration. "This guy's handwriting is crap," she complained. The inside corner of her mouth felt raw where she'd been chewing it. She absent-mindedly ran her tongue over the spot, soothing the sting.

Richard reached down and stroked a small stack of blue envelopes held together with a rubber band. "You want to pick something else?"

The clock read close to three in the morning, and she knew she had pushed him way past his limit. Sleep was about to have its way with both of them. She grudgingly accepted the fact that they probably couldn't make it any better. She made a decision.

"Let it fly like it is," she said.

She could see his body sag with relief. This wasn't their first criminal act, but if this whole thing went right, it could be their last.

"Hand it over."

Monica copied the message and saved it. Then she got on-line and pulled up the mail center. Carefully, she entered the correct e-mail address on the "To" line, and pasted the message in the big box like she had been shown. Richard loomed over her, studying the complex manipulations.

Satisfied that it looked correct, Monica's index finger still hesitated over the keyboard for a moment before she hit the send button.

"This better work or Steve really will have to come back from the dead."

Chapter 3

Clowns on the Wedding Cake

A courtroom was a sad place. If the walls could talk, they would cry. Judge Cross, the newest judge in the circuit, was given the oldest courtroom to work out of. No two chairs matched, the tables were scratched and wobbly, and the rug sported worn spots from years of shackled prisoners being shuffled back and forth.

It was just pure bad luck that Renee had gotten assigned to him. And talk about bad luck, Renee watched in dismay as Detective Graciano entered the public area and walked toward the state attorney's table.

"Boy, that man sure is fine," Sonja, Judge Cross's clerk, whispered. "Despite that geeky thing he's got going, he's a deluxe jumbo meal."

"Yeah, he's okay," Renee said, careful to keep her voice noncommittal. Her mouth tightened as she studied him, and her heart started a jittery dance. The man appeared even better looking than yesterday. He was unintentionally handsome and seemed hopelessly well adjusted. Something she'd never be.

"Just okay? Honey, if he don't light your fire, your wick is wet." Sonja shielded her mouth behind a file folder to keep the conversation private.

Renee's wick wasn't wet; it just hadn't been lit

in so long she forgot how to strike the matches. She watched the detective chat easily with the two attorneys that were representing the state of Florida today. "What's he doing here anyway? I've never seen him in this courtroom before."

Sonja starting stamping the date on a pile of case folders that threatened to topple off her desk. The old stamp hardly left a mark. "It's from the new mandate the chief judge handed down." Sonja wrinkled her nose in frustration and tried banging the stamp harder. "No more accepting the cops' written statements on murder cases, he wants live testimony only. Something to do with that last appeal. So, you'll be seeing more of the handsome detective from now on."

"Great. Just what I need," muttered Renee. "Why don't you try putting more ink in that thing?"

"You're a grump today. Don't have any. Have to requisition it, and that'll take months." She slammed the stamp again. "Anyway, he sure is easy on the eyes, girl." Sonja let out a huge, wistful sigh then lowered her voice. "Hell, I'd do him in the parking lot."

"Sure, he's nice looking, but so what? You remember my ex-husband, Kent?"

Sonja fanned herself, taking a break from punishing the folders. "Yeah, I remember him, so?"

"Nice looking, right?"

"Real fine. And your point is?"

"Good looking men are trouble. If I had known then what I know now, I would have put clowns on my wedding cake."

When Renee's marriage fell apart, it wasn't out of the blue. There had been signs all over the place. Big signs. Little signs. Signs Renee had ignored out of fear. She had refused to admit the future would involve lawyers, or acknowledge that that look on her husband's face was one of boredom, and maybe even a little revulsion that she couldn't let him go. Her husband hadn't only rejected their life together, he had rejected her. It had been a devastating blow as a wife, and as a woman. She had encased her heart like a miniature village in a snow globe; fragile but protected, and totally untouchable. She become a solo act and had been fine with it, until yesterday at Liz's when she had come alive for a moment. She had to admit it felt good, but it also scared the crap out of her.

Renee tapped her pearl-white fingernails on the table in annoyance. Detective Graciano had been in her thoughts all night, although she would never have admitted that to anyone. Against her better judgment, her long neglected sexual needs were being hauled out of dry dock.

She watched the people file in and find seats in the rows of creaky wooden benches. The crowd contained a mix of defendants, their lawyers, their family and friends, newspaper reporters and gawkers. This division handled all types of criminal matters, but mostly dealt with felonies. Felonies were the bigger crimes; murder, rape, armed robbery. A docket like this produced an endless stream of the dregs of society. The sour smell of fear and frustration wafted from the crowded gallery. For some, this was going to be the worst day of their lives. Over the years, Renee had seen it all, and frankly, she didn't think much of it.

Most of the staff was in a good mood today with Christmas being only a few days away. This was the last working day before a week-long holiday break. The sound of a steno case being wheeled down the aisle brought a frown to Renee's face. As the official court reporter in this courtroom, no other reporters were allowed for the criminal proceedings. When she saw it was Liz, she relaxed.

"What are you doing here?" Renee asked,

pleased to see her friend. Liz looked amazing, fresh and vibrant. If Renee hadn't known better, she would never have guessed that Liz had been up half the night drinking and looking at pictures of Steve. Renee knew, because she had been by her side. Renee stifled a yawn, hoping she looked half as good as her friend this morning. Liz wheeled up next to her and pulled over a chair.

"I lucked out," Liz said. "There are two private civil cases on this docket."

"On my criminal docket? No kidding? How did that happen?"

"My jobs cancelled for this morning, so the office started calling around, looking for open spots. You got an extra docket?" Liz started the process of unzipping, unfolding, and snapping, quickly setting up her machine.

A fresh batch of ICs—in custodys—people who were denied bail or couldn't make bail, were being settled and handcuffed to chairs in the empty jury box. Renee rearranged herself in an effort to keep her knees together. As a normal routine, she positioned the steno machine with the main support pole between her legs. This pleased the ICs, who were bored and had nothing better to do than sit over there and try to peek up her skirt. This morning's agenda contained thirteen names, a baker's dozen. According to the docket sheet, most of the hearings were scheduled for ten minutes each, except for the last one. Mostly it looked like a light day.

When Liz finally got settled, she started rummaging around in her purse. After pulling out a tampon, two ink pens, and a half-eaten candy bar, she solemnly handed Renee a crumpled wad of paper.

"I got another one this morning," Liz whispered.

Renee smoothed it out on her lap. It had only

three lines. Quick and to the point.

"Detective Graciano was just here a minute ago," Renee said, craning her neck to find him. Now he was nowhere around. "Where's a cop when you want one, huh?"

Renee studied her friend, weighing the impact her next question might have. Liz saw her look.

"What?"

"What if—" Renee faltered.

"What if what? Go ahead."

"What if Steve was still alive?" She gestured toward the back of the room where people were still making their way into the courtroom. "What if he walked through that door? What would you do?"

Liz bit her lower lip. "I've been asking myself that all night." Her face clouded as she focused on some inner private thought. "It would sure turn my world upside down after all I've been through." She turned to face her friend. "That sounds selfish, I know. And I'm embarrassed that that's my first reaction."

Renee touched Liz's arm. "You've had a tough year. Now you're thinking, okay, how much more do I have to take?" Renee looked at the copy of the e-mail and frowned. "It asks for money again." Her hope that it could be a prank was slipping away fast.

"I know. I spoke to Detective Slikowski a short time ago. She's sure someone is trying to con me into emptying my bank account, and that's exactly what I believe, too." Liz's mouth tightened in a harsh line. "How can somebody just crush my heart like this and not give a damn? Who would do something so ruthless, so cold?"

"Just look around you, are you kidding? For money?" Renee gestured to the assortment of flotsam and jetsam gathering in the courtroom.

"You're right. That bastard could be sitting in here right now watching me, gauging my reaction,"

Liz said bitterly.

The bailiff knocked on the wooden door to the anteroom three times and boomed, "All rise. The Circuit Court of the 29th Judicial Circuit is now in session. The Honorable Judge Wayne Cross presiding." Everyone scrambled to their feet and stood while the judge made his way up onto the bench and took his seat. He reached up and switched on a Christmas tree, a pitiful thing with some of the lights burnt out, and the star leaning to one side.

"You may be seated. Come to order and remain quiet."

Judge Cross appeared over the top of his bench, his right arm extended. "Ladies, are we ready?"

"Yes, Your Honor," Sonja replied. She snapped the case file in his hand like a nurse handing instruments to a surgeon.

She called the first case and the day began. The first one up was Liz's. The next two were Renee's. While Renee worked, Liz sat back in her chair with a bored look on her face, covertly checking her phone messages. Although interesting to the first-time observer, court reporters heard the same types of cases over and over and over again. It became mind numbing after a while.

When Renee's cases finished, the clerk began discussing scheduling issues with the judge, which gave everyone a few minutes break.

"What's that bit about topless in Massachusetts?" Renee asked, keeping her voice low. "Does that really mean something?"

"Yeah, it does. One summer night I was feeling frisky, and I took off my blouse and bra and sat up on the deck of Steve's convertible while he drove down a long, country road." Liz shook her head slowly. "I haven't the faintest idea how anybody would know that except Steve." Liz blew out a long, low breath, and bent low over her chair with her hands between her knees. "But that was years ago," she muttered, seemingly directing her comment to the carpet.

The clerk tapped the microphone and both reporters sat up straight and took a writing position in front of their machines. Renee stole a look over at her friend, but Liz's face was unreadable. Renee didn't know how long Liz could take this emotional beating. *That darn detective better do his job and find this creep.* After a short paper-shuffling pause, Sonja continued the criminal docket.

"Case #10-13205, Hanif Jafar."

Renee's head immediately jerked up. Oh, crap. She had forgotten all about him. Renee's mom took in a foreign exchange student each year. This year's student, a young man from Iran, had to travel earlier than originally planned because of some last minute visa mess up. Mom had gone on her annual Christmas cruise, so Renee agreed to take him in for the week. She had planned to have her day in court today covered so she could be home when he arrived, but with all the trauma at Liz's, she had completely forgotten about it. And now here he sat, an IC in the box. His first day in America. Just great.

Sitting in the middle of a row of degenerates, with his shiny hair and gorgeous dark complexion, he was easy to pick out. He didn't look scared, just genuinely baffled at what was happening. Renee felt terrible. Her stomach churned and the bitter after taste of this morning's coffee rolled around in her mouth. This was all her fault. It would be highly irregular for a court reporter to stand up and speak in the middle of a court proceeding. She would have to wait for a break to try and clear this up.

Judge Cross looked up from his paperwork. "What do we have here? Let me see his file." The judge tipped his head back and looked down his nose through his glasses at the contents. "Doesn't look like a major offender. What's this? The man's passport? He's a tourist? That's not going to sit well with our tourism board, now is it?"

"A couple ladies thought he could be a terrorist with the way he's dressed and his backpack, Your Honor." This came from the state attorney.

"Where are you?" the judge said, squinting at the jury box, using his hand to shield his eyes from the glare of the overhead lights. "Oh, there you are. Sit up, son, so we can see you." The judge shuffled through a bunch of papers. "So, what's the charge here? I can't seem to find the booking sheet."

"Disturbing the peace, Your Honor," the clerk replied. "He wouldn't leave the beach when told."

"Disturbing the peace? Isn't that a city violation? What's he doing in my courtroom?"

One of the public defenders stood. "You're one of the few judges left on today, Your Honor. Most are gone for the holidays. We were hoping we could get him arraigned in here. Otherwise, he'll have to wait until next week, and seeing as how it's Christmas this week, well, you know."

"I see. Okay. That's not a problem." The judge continued to study the file, making little notes on the edge of the booking sheet.

The bailiff piped up, "You also have three more small civil matters coming down from Judge Crenshaw's division, Your Honor."

"Well, we've got a mixed bag today, don't we?" Judge Cross murmured. He rubbed his eyes, then held the paper out in front of him at different lengths. He pulled off his glasses and wiped them with a tissue.

"We were hoping you would consider RORing him," the public defender added, "considering it's such a light charge."

That meant he'd be released on his own recognizance. No bail.

"Well, counselor," the judge slid his glasses back on and adjusted the left earpiece. "I can't do that without a proper address. How are we supposed to find him if he never shows up again? If he could perhaps give us an address, then maybe I would consider it. It's not much of a crime."

The judge addressed the prisoner directly. "Can you give us a local address where you'll be staying, sir?"

Hanif appeared to consider the judge's question for a few seconds, then sadly shook his head. "I can't remember it. It got changed at the last moment, and they took all my papers."

"You don't know anyone here? You don't have any friends here? No family?"

"I know this guy," Renee whispered to Liz, unable to hold it in any longer.

"Oh yeah? From where" Liz whispered back.

"I'll tell you later," she mouthed.

The judge peered over his bench at the pile of files waiting for him. "Okay, I can't waste any more time on this. I'll set bond for twenty-five dollars. Sir, all you have to do is come up with an address, a phone number, and twenty-five dollars and you can get out of jail. Otherwise, you'll have to be our guest until your case can be heard next week by the proper judge."

The clerk announced a short recess so the judge could take a phone call. Renee wanted to tell Hanif she knew he was there, but she couldn't. No one except attorneys could speak directly to the ICs.

Liz began packing her equipment.

"Where are you going?"

"The bailiff told me the civil cases just got sent down to Judge Miller instead. I'm going to head back to the office." Liz started to wheel away. "Let's order lunch from that new salad place," she said over her shoulder. "Call me when you're done."

"Sure, okay." As she watched Liz retreat down the aisle, Renee spotted someone she knew in the audience, Eddy, the bondsman.

"Sonja, how much time do we have? I need to talk to Eddy."

"You got at least ten minutes."

Renee headed over to where Eddy sat in the gallery. He smiled at her as she approached. Eddy Romano owned Bad Boyz Bonds. Under the phone number on his card, it read, "Cuz your mama wants you home." Rumor had it that Eddy's family was connected. In an Italian way. His dad was known as Joey the Realtor, because if Joey was looking for you, you were buying the farm.

"And good morning to you, Ms. Rose. What's up?"

"Eddy, look, I need to bail out this guy," Renee said, nodding toward the jury box.

"What guy?" Eddy tipped to the left to see around her. "You mean the terrorist? What, are you kiddin' me?"

"He's just a student from Iran that my mother is sponsoring. His transfer just got all screwed up is all." She found herself mimicking Eddy's speech mannerisms in an unconscious effort to win him over.

Eddy began to smirk. "Kind of young for you, ain't he?"

"Cut it out, Ed. I feel bad for him. Haven't you ever felt bad for somebody who was in trouble?"

Eddy thought about it for a moment before firmly answering. "No."

"Figures with your little itty-bitty heart. Come on," she said, her stomach churning at the mess she had caused for Hanif. He had been hanging around the beach waiting for her to come home. "Bail him out for me."

Once the paperwork had been processed, which

took forever, release time would be around eleven at night, which meant she'd have to wait outside the jail in the dark. If she didn't get robbed, raped, or car-jacked out there, she would collect him and take him home.

Renee continued to speak to Eddy, her voice soft, working him, because she knew Eddy wouldn't make enough money on this job to buy a coffee and it would strictly be a favor. "And anyway, I'm going to talk to the State. Maybe they'll drop the case. Did you see his sheet? It's a nothing charge. Hardly worth pursuing. Either way, it's my problem."

It would be her problem. She needed to get this charge dropped or he might not be able to stay in the United States. If she couldn't get it dropped, maybe she'd just haul him over to her mother's and say he took off. Let him get his schooling completed and go home. Of course, letting him go on the lam was against the law, aiding and abetting and all that. Although loitering on the beach wasn't exactly bank robber status.

"I'll steer some big time crook your way first chance I get," Renee said. "Promise."

"Okay, Ren, but I want cash. Get me the case number."

Renee retrieved her purse and the docket sheet. While she peeled off five-dollar bills, a man approached from her left and broke in on her dealings with Eddy.

"You're not going to pay that man's bond, are you?" he asked. His voice sounded raspy, but the incredulous tone rang clear. Then he fell into a coughing fit.

Renee bristled, annoyed at his intrusion, his tone, and his coughing close to her. She dismissed him with a back-handed wave. "If you're sick, you need to step away from me," she said, studying the bills in her hand. She handed them to Eddy.

"I'm not sick. I just swallowed wrong. And you shouldn't—"

"Do I know you?" she flung over her shoulder. "What concern is this of yours?" She turned to give the man a venomous look, a practiced look, a look many have backed off from, and—there he was. Detective Anthony-freakin'-Graciano.

Chapter 4

Stay

When Anthony drew closer, Renee could see he was a mess again. He had missed a spot shaving, his shirt looked rumpled, and his hair stuck out on one side. She peered into his green eyes and was annoyed at herself when a flash of heat coursed through her.

"Detective Graciano. From yesterday?" He held out his hand but quickly took it back when Renee ignored it.

She crossed her arms and faced him squarely. "I remember you, Detective. I'm not simple minded."

"Well, you're acting like it."

"I beg your pardon?" she said through clenched teeth.

"I see this kind of thing all the time. That man is a con, and he's taking advantage of you."

"You don't know that," Renee said, dismissing his advice, and him, by turning her back. She struggled to appear cool and in control. Despite being ticked off at his remark about her mental status, the nearness of him made her pulse race, and something was definitely going on with her knees. She handed Eddy the docket sheet and closed her purse with a sharp snap. "Why aren't you out working on Liz's case?" she flung over her shoulder. "Stay out of my business."

"Seeing people get fleeced is my business, Ms. Rose," he said. "I can't stop you from doing this, but if you don't really know Pretty Boy over there, you shouldn't get involved."

Renee barely controlled a shiver when he said her name. *What? Are we in high school now?* She struggled to bring herself under control, then turned and confronted the detective dead on.

"I didn't ask for a lecture. I have a father for that. I'll run my own life." He started to open his mouth, but she held up her hand. "Again, let me remind you it's none of your business." She kept her voice unfriendly but low, aware that they were a source of amusement to the people around them. "Why don't you concentrate on pulling *yourself* together?" She waggled her fingers at his crumpled shirt and hideous tie. "And leave me alone."

He put his hand to his chest as though he had been wounded, looked down at his clothes and did a quick survey. Apparently finding nothing wrong, he squared his shoulders. "It's my professional judgment that—"

"Is that the same judgment you use to pick out your ties?" Renee cut him off.

He clutched his tie with a protective tug. "Okay, lady. It's a free country. I just try to help when I see someone do something dumb."

She felt the warmth of an angry flush begin to creep across her face. "Detective, I'm not a wide-eyed innocent. You don't think I can tell a crook when I see one? I see the worst man has to offer every day. Some days it's so strong, I can almost taste it at lunch." She glared at him and pointed to the bench. "Go sit down and leave me alone."

Anthony backed off, hands up in surrender, and returned to his seat. He knew he had irritated her and that his tone had turned condescending, even though he had tried to sound professional and wise.

33

He wasn't sorry he'd interfered; this woman was acting stupid. Correction, this pretty woman was acting stupid. She had gotten to him yesterday. He couldn't put his finger on exactly what it was about her that made his blood run warmer, but to his dismay, he had spent much of the night thinking about her. He knew he should keep his mind on the bad guys and forget that woman. She felt all wrong for him. He had known from the moment he saw her in Liz's doorway she would be trouble. He had been immediately attracted to her and that was bad. She appeared independent and self assured. She laughed easily and exuded a confidence that meant she probably thought she didn't need a man. Definitely not his kind of woman. He preferred a damsel in distress. The distress part fit into the picture all right, but right now it came from his end.

He watched her as she finished up her interaction with the bondsman. She wasn't beautiful in the classic sense, like having porcelain skin, the girl-next-door look, or being dark and exotic. She mixed it up, and it was compelling. And she wasn't skinny like a lot of women these days. She was a real woman with curves that made his mouth go dry. He noticed the shape of her leg as she bent to show the man something on the docket. He liked the way her breasts moved when she walked. She wore a soft pink sweater over a black skirt. Nothing too tight or too short. Very conservative but also very sexy. He could hear the light rustle of her slip against her stockings. Black and lacy, it peeked out of the slit in her skirt. Her perfume lingered in his nostrils causing a light dizzying effect.

Anthony glanced over at the guy the court reporter was bailing out. He didn't look scared. As a cop, he had often seen innocent men squirm and fight back, and guilty ones curl up and fall asleep in the holding cell. It was hard to tell the innocence or guilt of someone, and in his experience, most everyone will lie when they find themselves in trouble. She had said he was a student. That didn't make him an angel. It would be better all around if the court reporter just let this guy work out his own problems.

A moment later, Anthony saw her look his way, and even though it wasn't a very friendly glance, his heart stuttered. He couldn't remember the last time a woman made him feel that way. She ran her hand through her dark hair and laughed at something the bondsman said. Her earrings sparkled from the overhead lights. He forced himself to study his shoes and not stare. He should ignore her and stay out of her business, just like she asked him to.

It would be just his unfortunate luck to become infatuated with someone like Madam Court Reporter over there. He watched her for another moment, shook his head in resignation, and started to get up, willing and wanting to try to reason with her one more time.

"You know…" he started.

Renee turned quickly, pointed a finger at him, and said sharply, "Stay." Just like a dog. And he did.

Chapter 5

Out for Coffee and Donuts

Monica worried about the manager coming to the room.

"Rich, for God's sake shut up," she begged. "The walls in this dump are friggin' thin."

Why Richard hadn't stayed in his drug-induced coma most of the day was a mystery. That's what she had planned to do.

She cast a bleary eye at the clock. "It's not even noon," she wailed. "Go back to bed."

"I want out of this miserable, hot, stinkin' town," he complained.

"There's the door," Monica said wearily.

"Oh, you'd love that, wouldn't you?" he yelled. "Then you'd have all that money to yourself."

"Maybe you could say that a little louder. I don't think the guy in the corner room heard you."

Sitting with her legs hanging over the side of the bed, she alternated between raising one hand in a weak attempt at a shushing motion and holding her throbbing head securely on her neck with both hands afraid it might fall off and roll under the bed.

The hot burn of bile rose in her throat. Clutching her stomach, she groaned and flopped back on the bed. If they were thrown out of the motel, she wasn't sure she could make it down the street to the next flop house. She wasn't even sure she could make it to the bathroom. He had to be calmed down. How to do that was a little fuzzy. She wiped her nose on her arm and watched him stomp around the room like a maniac, rambling on about his life and his ex-wife and things she didn't even understand.

"Look, what's your problem, dude? We got a plan. We just gotta stick to it."

"She ain't gonna fall for that crap. This whole thing is stupid." Richard slammed his fist on the table. It teetered on one side before righting itself. "I ain't going to jail again."

Monica wondered if he was one of them schizophrenic people. Or maybe he had that polar bear disease, up one day and down the next. Whatever he had, it was annoying and wearing on her last nerve.

"I hate this shitty end of town. I hate this ratty old motel." He threw a half empty soda can with enough force that it sprayed when it hit the wall.

"You're just hungry, go get some food," she suggested, blinking furiously. Her left eye started to water and she couldn't seem to get it to focus.

He stopped in his tracks. "Now that's a good idea." He pointed a finger in her direction. "I'm going out for donuts and coffee."

"Yeah, that's swell," she nodded. "Ouch." She abruptly stopped moving her head. "Coffee. Lots of coffee."

"Why don't you clean yourself up when I'm gone?" He wrinkled his nose and looked down at her. "You're a mess."

She knew she wasn't the freshest daisy in the bunch. Most days she didn't care.

"Yeah, yeah, okay," she readily agreed just to shut him up. "You go out for a bit and I'll take a shower."

He slipped into his shoes and ran a hand

through his own greasy hair.

"Get me Boston cream." She held up two fingers, "Two of 'em."

When Richard left, Monica fell straight back into bed. The relief of sleep came immediately. The next time she opened her eyes, the clock read four p.m. The room was wonderfully empty, and quiet.

"Where the hell's my coffee?" she croaked.

A phlegmy coughing fit brought black dots whirling around her head. Richard was nowhere to be seen. The top of the dresser where his meager possessions had been parked was conspicuously empty. A peek in the bathroom revealed that his shaving crap was also gone. He had taken his wallet, which Monica knew had a pitiful fourteen dollars in it.

"Well, good riddance to a bad penny." She dragged herself out of bed. "I don't need you, you bum," she yelled to the closed front door. "I'm the brains of the litter anyways." She teetered into the bathroom and splashed cold water on her face.

"I need a cigarette," she muttered. Turning back into the bedroom area, she froze mid stagger to stare at the bare spot on the nightstand. The cardboard box that held the computer and letters was gone.

"That son of a bitch," Monica screeched. She ran to the front door, but he was long gone. "That son of a bitch," she repeated. She slammed the door and threw herself against it. Tears stung her eyes.

"He can't get away with this", she said to the empty room. Furious, she threw on some clothes and went in search of her not-so-hot boyfriend. She walked up and down the beach road, not sure which way he might have headed. He had no home, no car, and no place to go. She sat on the seawall to gather her thoughts. A hung-over barmaid, her makeup smeared, her uniform looking clownish in the daylight made her way along the cracked sidewalk.

She had several dark bruises on one arm. Monica watched her lurch by when it hit her.

"I hate this shitty end of town. That's what he said."

She glanced down the long avenue to the other end of the beach where rents were tripled and art galleries mixed in with trendy boutiques.

"That's where you are, all right," she said to herself, positive he had gotten himself down to the ritzy end of the beach away from the crappy run-down motels, away from the tourist bars that were shabby in the light of day, away from the flimflam artists and T-shirt shops. He was a flimflam man himself and he wouldn't fit in, but maybe he would pretend to be a tourist. She'd find him. If it took her last breath, she'd find him. And when she did, he wouldn't be sending any more e-mails to anybody.

Chapter 6

One Black Sock, One Blue

Renee's last case of the morning was a defense motion to suppress. The participants assembled at their respective tables. Sonja called the first witness. When she announced the name, Renee mentally rolled her eyes. As Detective Graciano passed the wooden bar that separated the court personnel from where the public sat and neared her area, she became aggravated to find that her pulse quickened. Under the pretense of checking the paper supply in her machine's tray, she busied herself, determined to keep a calm exterior and not let him or anyone else see the reaction he caused in her just by walking by. It was embarrassing, really.

Detective Graciano gave Renee a little nod as he moved past her and climbed into the witness box. Renee didn't respond, but as she watched his progression, she realized something seemed off. He moved slowly and barely raised his hand when sworn in. He sat way back in his chair, legs sprawled, with an almost bored look on his face. His feet stuck out of the bottom of the witness stand. Renee stared at his socks and shook her head. One blue, one black.

Attorney Ryan approached the podium with a yellow legal pad. "Please state your name for the record, Detective."

Renee's fingers moved quietly over the keyboard.

"Anthony Mar—" then his voice faded.

Renee's fingers stopped. "I'm sorry?"

The detective looked down at her from the witness stand with a puzzled look on his face. "For what?"

"I couldn't hear you," Renee said.

"Could you speak up for the court reporter, please?" Attorney Ryan suggested.

"Sure," Anthony said, shrugging his shoulders and flopping back in his seat. He furrowed his forehead and appeared to be concentrating.

Everyone waited a few heartbeats. Renee looked over at the defense attorney and raised her eyebrows in a question.

"Could you repeat your name, Detective?" Ryan said patiently.

The detective let out a big sigh, took a deep breath, and boomed loudly into the mike making everyone jump. "Anthony Martin Graciano."

"Where do you work, Detective?"

Renee knew he worked out of JPD, Jacaranda Police Department, but she could hardly hear it. She wrote it anyway, starting to become annoyed. Now he had his hands in front of his face and he rubbed his eyes.

"And how long have you been with JPD?" Ryan asked.

"A very long time, over two mummmmm years."

Renee didn't get the answer. She quickly made a note to ask later. She'd have to fill it in. This went on for about five more questions before she grew irritated enough to speak up to the judge.

"Your Honor, the court reporter cannot hear this witness. Would you please instruct him to answer clearly?"

Judge Cross leaned over the bench and glared at

Anthony. "Detective, I don't know what your problem is here this morning, but it's not appreciated in my courtroom. You will answer all the questions clearly and speak directly into the mike so the court reporter can get an accurate record. Is that understood?"

Detective Graciano shot Renee a withering look as he leaned forward and adjusted the mike so it sat perfectly under his nose. "Yes, Your Honor. I apologize. I was up all night, got called out on a case, but I got this subpoena to be here this morning to testify and the state would not release me, so I had to honor it, Your Honor it."

Renee frowned down at her machine. Did he just say honor it, your honor it? She didn't have time to think about it, because the defense attorney raised an objection as to the accuracy of the witness's memory in his present condition and his ability to testify. A five-minute argument ensued, which meant everyone talked quickly and interrupted each other. Renee shifted into overdrive and dutifully recorded everything. The defense attorney asked for a moment to find a piece of information requested by the judge. Renee shook out her hands, glanced up at the witness stand, and let out a little gasp. He had fallen asleep in his chair. Attorney Ryan, shaking a fistful of papers, was conferring with a colleague. Renee caught his eye and nodded her head toward the witness stand. Ryan threw his hands up in the air. A few of his papers broke loose and fluttered around the table.

"Your Honor?" he said, pointing at the detective, his voice rising into a whine.

Judge Cross stood up and peered over and down at the sleeping detective. Tittering and laughter filtered up from the gallery. The judge settled himself back in his comfortable but frayed chair, adjusted his robe, and listened to arguments about rescheduling the hearing before granting the motion.

A court officer shook Detective Graciano awake and he came to with a start. A few uncomfortable moments passed while he stood hands clasped behind his back and head slightly bowed before the judge who gave him a stern lecture on witness decorum. Even though he was a pain, Renee felt bad for him.

The courtroom cleared out when Judge Cross recessed for a thirty-minute break. Sonja started calling around to see if the judge could pick up another hearing or short trial, seeing as how this one washed out freeing up almost two hours. Renee took a moment to make a few notes and label her computer file, then she headed for the coffee shop across the square. As she stepped off the curb, she spied Detective Graciano on the opposite corner talking to Gene, the homeless man who hung around the courthouse block. She watched as the detective dug out his wallet, opened it, and counted out several bills. When he handed them to Gene, he was rewarded with a dark, toothless smile. They spoke amiably for a few moments, like any two normal friends who might meet on a corner, before Gene shuffled off, one wheel of his rusted grocery cart precariously wobbling under the load.

The café stood almost empty at this time of day. Renee ordered a vanilla latte, her favorite, and mulled over the detective's kindness. She left the shop determined to try to be nicer to him but her decision was short lived when he grabbed her elbow a moment later and hot coffee splashed over her fingers.

"What happened in there?" Anthony demanded.

With only a slight move of her head, Renee stared down at his hand then up into his eyes.

"Sorry," he said, quickly raising both of his arms in a hands-up gesture. "I just wanted to catch you before you crossed the street."

Close enough to feel the heat of his body, Renee found herself drawn to it. His cologne smelled expensive and heady; maybe a gift from his partner because it didn't match the rest of him. A little flash of electricity zinged through her. Annoyed at herself, she quickly shook it off. The last thing she needed was to start having twinges where it mattered for a cop.

"You didn't have to make me look bad."

"I made you look bad?" Renee said incredulously. "You fell asleep on the witness stand in the middle of your testimony." She shook her hand but the sticky drops of latte wouldn't come off. "In front of everybody," she added. "How is it that I made you look bad?"

"I just rested my eyes for a second," he protested vehemently.

"Uh-huh, of course you did." Renee patted him lightly on the arm leaving a smudge of brown on his jacket.

"If you hadn't interrupted me, I could have gotten my testimony out and it would be done with," he grumbled. "But nooo, you had to complain. You were just miffed because I tried to help you before." He flung the accusation at her, but his eyes said he knew it sounded lame.

"I couldn't hear you. What was I supposed to do, just make stuff up?" She pinned him in place with her glare. "And another thing, I didn't ask for your opinion about the IC. I didn't ask for it and I don't need it."

That spot he had missed while shaving looked even darker outdoors. Renee had a difficult time not staring at it.

He pointed his finger. "You shouldn't get yourself involved with a low life."

"What are you, my big brother now? I'm in

control of the situation, thank you very much. And don't you point your finger at me," she said, slapping it away. "You know, you need to work on your personality. You have none."

Her heart beat a little thump of protest at how hard she was being on him. She blew out a frustrated breath and made an effort to soften her voice. "Can I go back to work now, Detective? I mean if you're done bossing me around, that is."

****

Anthony couldn't think of any way to salvage this conversation. He had been bossing her around, and even though she stood a few inches shorter than he, she had faced him and hadn't backed down. Now she had a hand on her waist, with her head doing that female shaky thing women do when they're mad. He stepped aside and let her pass, watching her walk across the street, appreciating the swing of her hips. His mind drifted back to that lacey slip. *What else was she wearing that was black?*

"I hope I never have to be in court with you again," he called after her, desperate to salvage his manhood with the last word, but regretting it the moment it came out of his mouth.

"Works for me," she shot back over her shoulder.

"I'm an idiot," he muttered. She wasn't his type anyway, so what did it matter? Although, it had struck him that she had the prettiest eyes he'd ever seen. In the sunlight they were like stained glass, changing from blue to green. He turned and stalked off toward the parking lot, angrily kicking a palm frond out of his way.

"She makes me crazy," Anthony lamented to no one in particular. A car pulled up to the curb next to him. The passenger door slowly opened.

"Get in," a female voice called out to him.

He lumbered to the car and climbed in. "Grace, if you say one word, I swear I'll pull my weapon and kill myself." He made a half-hearted attempt to straighten his jacket. "I swear it."

Slikowski bit her lip, an apparent attempt to keep from snorting with laughter. She kept her hands on the wheel, eyes forward. "Close the door there, Brilliance, and I'll take you home. You need some sleep."

Anthony pulled the door shut and slunk back in his seat. When he glanced down at his feet, he let out a little moan. Mortified that his socks didn't match, he flopped his head to the side and let it smack against the window. The car pulled away and into traffic.

He fingered his tie. "Grace, do you think this is a bad tie?"

She grinned over at him. "You like her," she stated matter-of-factly.

Anthony quickly changed the subject. "Don't even start on me about the seat belt, Slicky. I don't have the strength."

The best thing would be to forget all about that woman. She already caused him grief. So, he had just gotten sliced and diced. Big deal. But he felt surprised to find he was experiencing an emotion that felt a lot like disappointment. There was no reason to be disappointed because he didn't inspire flaming passion in the woman. After all, she told him flat out to get lost. Yeah, she sure did. He let that slosh around him like dirty water at the bottom of a boat.

He rubbed hard at his eyes. He flopped back against the headrest and watched little black dots dance around the car.

Today had been a warning shot to his heart. A smart man would go home, go to bed, and put that court reporter out of his mind. A smart man would solve her friend's case and then wash his hands of her.

A smart man might even assign the case to someone else.

Oh, hell. Anthony knew he wasn't all that smart.

Chapter 7

A Lifting Machine

Court reporting wasn't really a career. It was more like a punishment. On any given day, Renee came into contact with an endless parade of murderers, rapists, and thieves. That had been a huge part of the reason she moved into a high-rise condo along the ocean with the twenty-four hour guard service and gated garage. Renee parked her car, looking forward to the cool, calm interior of her condo, dragged her case out of the trunk, and walked into the lobby heading toward the mail room. She waved to Ramon, the day guard, as she passed by the security area.

"Hey, Ms. Rose. How ya' doing?" Ramon called out from the doorway to his office. "By the way, some guy was here looking for you this morning. Didn't leave his name. Looked a little shady, you ask me."

Ramon reached over and tapped one of the security screens. The black face of the monitor flickered a few times before the parking garage came into view.

"Hey, there he is. Look, across the driveway there, that's him."

Renee felt relieved to see the Iranian student sitting on the rocks by the flowerbed. Now she wouldn't have to go disentangle him from the rest of the flotsam and jetsam tonight at release time, not to mention suffer the remarks, assorted passes, and fabulous offers she would be sure to get at the jail. She crossed the driveway to where he sat patiently waiting.

"Hanif?"

He rose and gave her what appeared to be a genuinely happy smile, considering he had just been in the hoosegow.

"How did you get out so fast? That never happens."

"They said to have a nice Christmas and they let me out."

"Okay, good. Well, you're in the right spot. I'm Renee, you'll be staying with me this week."

Renee turned on her heel and led him back to the front entrance. She held the door open and nodded toward the inside.

"I am so thankful to you and your mother," Hanif said, stepping into the lobby. He looked around appreciatively, taking in the glass tables, paintings along the walls, and the soft, leather sofas. A far cry from where he had been this morning.

"Yeah, well, you haven't tasted my cooking yet." She began to gather her belongings that she had dropped in the lobby. "I'm sorry about the court thing. I got you out soon as I could."

"No, it is I who am sorry. I did not mean to break any of your laws. I will be more careful," he said, a solemn look on his face. "I promise."

He clutched his backpack tightly to his chest, his only piece of luggage. All the way from Iran, staying here and going to school for six months at the very least, and all he owned fit in one little bag. Renee had more stuff going to work every day.

Mom used the same student program every year and there had never been a problem. The exchange people did a hell of a good job screening their applicants and Renee felt confident Hanif was just as he appeared, a traveling foreign student, but she decided to give herself a little extra insurance. After all, she didn't really know this guy. As soon as that thought surfaced, a clear picture of Detective Graciano's disapproving face popped into her head. She brushed it aside with an irritated mental sweep. She pointed over to Ramon.

"See that guy? All I have to do is call him and he'll come up and remove you. You won't give me any trouble, right?"

"Never," Hanif vowed vehemently, peering uneasily over at Ramon. "I would never give you trouble."

"Then, in a week, you'll be out of my hair and at my mom's, okay?"

Hanif took a step back and studied her head warily. "I would never be in your hair," he said slowly.

Renee felt glad he didn't understand what she just said. Sometimes she was too blunt. She had been an only child born to a father who desperately wanted a son and never let her forget how she had let him down. As many little girls do, Renee married a man like her father, and then proceeded to wear herself out trying to please him. It took ten years for her to realize she could never have pleased either of them, and it wasn't her fault. It made her stronger, but harder. It was something she had to work on.

She smiled, trying to make him feel comfortable. "That's just an expression. I don't mind you staying here," she added. "Really." She handed him her heavy transcript bag. "Start being useful."

She went over to the elevator and punched a button. The doors whisked open but Hanif stayed in the middle of the lobby.

"Are you coming or not?" she called over to him.

"Uh, yes. I'm coming. Over there?"

"Duh, yes." She rolled her eyes at him in a

teasing manner. "Unless you want to climb up ten flights of stairs."

He walked over and stepped into the box, facing her, his reflection in the mirrored walls showcasing a full head of shiny, dark hair.

Renee pointed to the panel by the doors. "Press the button marked ten." When they started moving, Hanif's eyes widened and a grin split his face.

"It's a lifting machine," he said. "I have heard of such things."

"Elevator. We say elevator here."

This next week was going to be very interesting.

Renee went through the door first, lugging her computer case, handbag, and this morning's travel coffee mug. She dumped the heavy stuff by the door and placed the mug in the sink.

"What's this called?" He pointed to the security alarm box. "And this?" The coffee maker. He wandered all over her apartment, touching things, examining things, and opening things. Everyday items, stuff she took for granted, were all new to him. Leaning against the counter with her arms crossed, she watched, amused, explaining as best she could.

After a while, when he began to wear her out, she rolled her machine into her office and dumped today's jobs into her desk top computer.

At this point, he had worked his way into the bathroom. The fact that he could get water by just touching the faucet floored him. Literally. He sat on the bathroom floor, his hands exploring the tub.

"Get up from there," Renee complained. "God knows when I last mopped that." She began to get a picture of this guy's life. "How did you get your schooling back in Iran?" she asked.

"I walked many miles across the desert each day to attend school. It was in a tent, but it had electricity and a satellite dish. Much of my work was done on the computer. I went to that school because they taught English there. It was most advanced for the area."

Renee creased her brow. "A tent, huh? But I've seen pictures of Tehran, it's a huge, beautiful city surrounded by mountains."

"Yes, it is, but I have never been to it. I live hundreds of miles to the south, in the desert at Dasht-e-Kavfir. It's the hottest area on Earth, they say. My people are nomads, moving around from place to place to find water and plant life for the animals. That's why I want to learn to construct desalination plants." His face glowed with the possibility. "When I go back, I plan to flood the desert with water and make south Iran a lush, green garden."

He turned on the faucet and let the water run over his hands. "Everyone will be able to do this." He smiled broadly. "Even the poorest of us."

The ringing of the phone shattered their fun. Liz had received another e-mail.

Chapter 8

A Walking Pile of Rags

"He ain't keep up wid his hygienes, ya know what I'm saying?"

"Yeah, we hear you, Paulie." Detective Graciano wrinkled his nose and took a step to the right in an effort to keep upwind of the bum. Grace appeared to be trying to stand her ground and grimly took notes.

"So besides his smell, can you tell us anything else about the guy?" she asked, breathing through her mouth.

The bum picked a bottle out of the trash and grinned, exposing three loose teeth. "This here's worth five cent." He looked around nervously before covertly stuffing it under a mound of plastic bags in his shopping cart.

Grace tapped the pen on her pad in a quick rhythm and rolled her eyes. "We're wasting our time here," she muttered, looking over at Anthony who had put a distance between himself and the odorous bum. "You working this or what?" she shot at him.

Anthony had been thinking about the court reporter. The woman had gotten to him. He couldn't put his finger on exactly what it was about her that made his blood run warmer, but he couldn't stop thinking about her. He had to keep his mind on the bad guys and forget that woman. He didn't want a relationship, didn't need one, and sure as shit didn't deserve one. Besides, she was all wrong for him.

He moved closer and lowered his head to peer into the bum's face. "Concentrate, Paulie. What else can you tell us beside what the guy smelled like? Was he white, black, Hispanic, Martian?"

"He a white guy, but that's all I kin tell ya. Y'all look alike to me," he grumbled.

Anthony looked over at Grace's notepad. Besides the date and alleged crime, it contained only three words; bummy, white male. "Not much to go on," he complained. "Anything else you can remember about him," he prodded.

"Ain't nothin' else ta say. Like I tole ya, he went into that fancy airport diner over there and walked out with the guy's silver computer under his arm pretty as you please."

"And you're sure he didn't have it walking in, right?" Anthony asked.

"Course I'm sure. I tole ya that, didn't I? I seen him. This my territory, ya know? My neighborhood. I pick this trash right here. This be my career. I ain't let nobody mess wid my career. I be watching evra' body and evra' thing, ya hear me? When I seen that, I jest laugh and laugh. He be real slick. Jest like Slicky here," he grinned, pointing a dirty finger at Grace.

Grace narrowed her eyes and glared at Anthony. Slicky was a nickname Anthony had given her soon after they had partnered up. Now it seemed to be everywhere, even down here in the gutter. She put her hand on her stun gun and looked like she was considering the ramifications of giving Anthony a quick jolt.

Anthony backed up, hands in the air, a smirk across his face. "I swear to God. I swear to God, Detective Slikowski, I never told him that."

Grace didn't blink. She released the latch on her holster with her thumb.

"Really. Honest," Anthony added quickly. He turned toward Paulie and wagged his finger. "Let me just remind you," he said sternly, having trouble holding in his laughter, "that it's Detective Slikowski. A little respect for law enforcement."

The bum peered over at Grace, studied her for a moment, lost interest, then went back to the trash can. "She ain't got no uniform," he muttered, wiping his nose on his sleeve.

"Come on, Grace, lighten up for Chrissakes." Anthony grinned. He pulled out his wallet. "Next time don't wait two days to tell us, Paulie." He extended a ten-dollar bill toward the ratty little man. A little reward for being a good citizen and reporting a theft. One of the many things Anthony did contrary to departmental policy. Things like speeding, turning his head at minor infractions, and not only looking the other way if a homeless guy is sleeping on a park bench, but sticking a twenty in his pocket. A department psychologist once told him the reason he rebelled in trivial ways was because of his anger at the fact that he always had to be the good guy, always had to protect everyone.

Paulie quickly stuffed the bill into one of his socks.

"Everybody knows you as Slicky," Anthony said. "It's a small town."

"Yeah, yeah, yeah," Grace said. "I just hate handling these petty-ass calls."

Being two of only four detectives in a small police force required that Grace and Anthony cover jobs that most agencies would have a patrol officer handle. It also required them to work closely together for long hours. Anthony handled it better than Grace. For him, it had always been the job. Always. He both loved it and hated it, but he needed it. Here he was back out on the street after less than six hours of sleep.

Paulie rummaged around the trash can in earnest for a few seconds then wandered away, a moving pile of rags.

Anthony shook his head. "Come on, we're done here."

"Sometimes I wonder if he has any tomatoes in his salad," Grace said. She flipped her notepad closed and carefully picked her way out of the alley.

Chapter 9

It's Raining Men

"Did you call the detectives?" Renee asked Liz, cradling the kitchen phone against her ear. She poured two glasses of orange juice and passed one over the counter to Hanif. Stormy, her male cat, sat on the counter watching her intently. When Renee scratched him under his chin, he closed his eyes in ecstasy and began drooling. If only all men were that easy.

"Yes, they're on their way."

"Couldn't you just forward the new e-mail to them?" After this morning, Renee had decided to try to never have contact with Anthony Graciano again, and here he was a side dish on tonight's dinner menu.

"Detective Graciano said he wanted to stop by and show me something. He also asked if you would be here," Liz added, holding the word "you" a beat longer than necessary.

Renee took a sip of juice and wondered why she wasn't more unhappy. She'd have to work on keeping her defenses up, because if she let him, Detective Graciano could sure show her something all right.

A noise brought her back to the present, and away from the thought of dimples. Hanif gulped down his juice making loud slurping sounds.

"Take it easy. No, not you, Liz," Renee said into the mouthpiece. "I have a visitor, and he's choking on orange juice."

"He?" Liz asked, her voice rising with interest.

"I'll bring him along and explain when we get there."

"Oooh, there's explaining to be done. I love it. Hurry over."

"We'll be there in half an hour. Call Lee Fong's and I'll pick up Chinese on the way."

Renee hung up and stared hard at Hanif, who was finishing his OJ with obvious delight. She rubbed her forehead where a little headache had begun to form. Her heretofore simple, quiet life had gotten complicated. Suddenly it was raining men.

Hanif tipped the glass back to get every drop. "This is great stuff."

"You've never had orange juice before?" Renee smiled. This guy was rather entertaining. She took the empty glass and took it over to the sink. "You should try this with vodka. Never mind. We have to go over to my friend, Liz's, now."

She studied Hanif. His dark, slightly unruly, hair just hit his collar. He had deep, almost black, eyes, and his skin had a wonderful olive tone. His features were strong, his lips full. She took in his dark, traditional Iranian loose trousers, long white tunic, and brown vest. If he had a turban, he could definitely pass for a terrorist.

"I'm going to dig out some old sweats for you. Your clothes make you stand out." Renee headed into her closet and rummaged around a moment before pulling out a storage box filled with gray and blue running clothes. The smell of her ex-husband wafted up, a mixture of his cologne and natural body. She resisted the urge to pull the soft material to her face and inhale.

"These are all that's left of my marriage," she

said softly. "I should have dumped these things a long time ago."

She pulled pants and T-shirts out until she found something she was happy with. "Good, here's a pair of flip-flops, too." She handed the pile to Hanif. "Change into these."

When Hanif emerged from the bathroom, he looked normal, very American male. Renee took a peek behind him. His clothes were on the bathroom floor in a heap. Apparently, some things were universal.

"Much better. Now we have to pick up Chinese and get over to Liz's."

"Okay." He sat on the couch and wiggled his feet into his new shoes. He made a face but left them on. "Who is Liz?"

"She's my best friend. She's having a little domestic problem right now, and she needs me to hold her hand."

"Hold her hand? Really?" Hanif's eyebrows were drawn together in question. "What good would that do?"

"Well, not hold her hand in the physical sense, but be there for her, you know? It's an expression here." Renee turned out the lights and grabbed her purse. Hanif still sat on the couch.

"You coming or what?" Renee said.

"Or what?"

"That's another expression. Come on."

Hanif flip-flopped unsteadily to the elevator. "These are like wearing nothing," he complained, stepping through the doors when they opened.

"Yeah, that's the beauty of them. Great, aren't they? Come on, I'm parked toward the back of the lot."

Hanif had a hard time figuring out how to get in the car. He was all thumbs with the seat belt. He studied the dashboard as though he were memorizing it. He pushed buttons, opened the glove box, and turned the makeup light on. And all this before they even left the garage.

"Will you stop that," Renee said, closing the ashtray with a decisive snap. "I have all my settings where I want them."

Hanif turned in his seat toward her. "What's a setting?"

Chapter 10

Good Cop / Bad Cop and Chinese Food

The detectives had arrived before Renee and Hanif reached Liz's house. Renee could see Anthony through the front window and suddenly her blood felt warmer in her veins. *Damn him, he looked good.* He kept a wary eye out as Beans danced around, trying to get Detective Slikowski's attention. The moment Renee and Hanif entered, Detective Graciano rapidly crossed the room and stood before them, his back rigid.

"What is he doing here?" he barked. Before Renee could open her mouth, the detective hustled her aside and lowered his voice. His manner was brusque and irritating, but nevertheless, she found his nearness alarming. Parts of her that had been dormant for years were stirring. He smelled wonderful, and Renee fought the urge to lean closer. Just a few more inches, and she could nibble his neck. This was bad. Trying to distract herself and get some emotional distance from him, she looked him up and down critically. He had on a pair of jeans and a sports jacket. At least he hadn't worn an awful tie.

"You must be working plain clothes tonight," she observed.

"No, I'm not," he said, pulling his sleeve cuffs out with a sharp tug. "Don't change the subject."

"Oh, sorry," she said, clearly not.

"Answer my question."

Not one to be scolded into submission, Renee jutted her chin out in a defiant manner. "Hanif's with me. Is that a problem, Detective?"

"Yeah, it's a problem. He's a con. What are you doing hanging around a bum like that for? What in hell are you thinking? Don't you—"

"Wait just one darn minute. You don't know this guy. How dare you—"

"And you don't know him either," Anthony interrupted, making a gesture like he'd like to strangle her. He set his jaw, his hard face all business. "I don't have to know him personally to know his kind. Just look at him." They both looked over to where Hanif stood examining a sad little plant that sprouted two tiny leaves in a silly fit of optimism. Silk greenery filled the rest of the house. And a good thing, too. Liz was a bona fide, black thumb, plant killer.

"Yeah, he's a real sociopath," Renee said. "No, you look at him. You deal with crooks every day. Does he look like a maniac to you? He's a student. He's going to—you know what? It's none of your business. What do you care, anyway? Leave it alone."

Renee still held the box of Chinese food. The smell filled the room. Her stomach growled.

"Okay, I'll drop it for now," Anthony said, apparently trying a new tact as his voice became calmer, friendlier. "But this isn't over by a long shot."

Renee stared at his crooked smile with suspicion. "When you do good cop/bad cop, aren't there supposed to be two of you?"

He glanced down at the collection of little brown bags stapled on the top. "Did you bring enough for me?"

Renee put a protective hand over the bags. "You were not invited."

"Oh, yes, I was," he said, pointing to Liz. His smile worked those dimples, and those dimples worked on Renee. She pulled herself away by sheer will and went over to greet her friend, who had just come in from putting Beans in the backyard. Liz's face appeared blotchy. She must have been crying before everyone got there.

"How're you holding up?" Renee asked, bringing the take-out into the kitchen area and placing the box on the counter. Liz's tiny kitchen opened into the dining room leaving no chance for a private conversation. Liz gave her a dismissive wave. "I'll be fine. I'll be better with some food in me. I'm starving." She gestured toward the computer. "I know it's not Steve. It's just so hurtful of someone to do this."

Hanif had stopped his inspection of the plant and now peered into the bags on the counter. Liz's eyes widened in a question, and a small grin spread over her face.

"Liz, this is Hanif." Renee lowered her voice to barely a whisper. "And yes, it's the guy from court this morning, and no, I don't want to talk about it right now." Renee tipped her head toward the front door where Anthony talked to his partner. Liz leaned in and whispered back, "I heard a story about Detective Graciano this afternoon, about why he acts the way he does. Remind me to tell you later."

She straightened up and pointed to a cupboard. "Hanif, the plates are up there. Here's a pitcher of iced tea. Help yourself and have a seat. I have to finish up with Detective Slikowski."

Liz walked over to where her computer sat and tapped a few keys. Detective Slikowski read the new e-mail, then printed out the latest message.

In four days, I will get my chance. Will explain

all when I see you. Will need $50,000 cash to bribe guard and driver. Plans will be in place tomorrow. Will send instructions for drop off point.

Love, Steve.

P.S. Blue dive fins at the restaurant.

Detective Slikowski informed Liz that the e-mails were coming from a stolen laptop that belonged to a guy named Earl Russell in Chicago. She flipped through a folder and pulled out a piece of paper. "Mr. Russell's story checks out, but take a look at his DMV photo anyway. Do you recognize him?" Detective Graciano asked. Both Liz and Renee confirmed that they had never heard of Earl Russell and did not know the man in the driver's license photo.

"An inquiry to the online server produced information that the first two e-mails were sent locally. Probably this one, too. They can't tell us the address though," Detective Slikowski said. "They're keeping Russell's account up and running to aid us in this investigation."

Liz's face dropped into a frown. "They're local? These guys are right here?" She folded her arms and hugged herself. "I don't like that. When this started, because it was on the computer, I thought it was coming from—" She stopped. "I don't know exactly where I thought it was coming from, but not right here in Jacaranda."

"Do you have somebody you can stay with for the next few days? I don't think it's a good idea to stay alone." This piece of advice came from Detective Graciano.

"Of course she has someplace to stay," Renee said, shooting him a disgusted look before moving around the table to give Liz a comforting hug. "I'm her best friend, for heaven's sake."

Detective Graciano shot Hanif a look. "That may be, but you have him."

"And your point is?" Renee retorted.

"That's it. That's my point," Anthony said, giving her a hard look.

Detective Slikowksi stepped between the two of them and stared at Anthony. "Ind-may your own usiness-bay," she mouthed to Anthony. He backed away and sat on the edge of the couch.

"Listen, Ms. Sutton," Detective Slikowski said. "In the first two e-mails, the bad guys just hinted at needing money. Now they've made a specific dollar amount demand and said drop-off info was coming. And we know they're local. This case just went from a hurtful prank to serious criminal activity. You keep in touch if any new e-mails or other contacts are made, and let us know where you're going to be, all right?"

Liz agreed and slumped down at the dining room table, visibly upset at the new development. Renee made a silent vow to try to be civil to Detective Graciano. This was not the time to bring bickering into the house. She sat at the other end of the table, putting something solid between her and Anthony.

"Who knew about the insurance money coming in this month?" Detective Graciano asked Liz.

"Well, Renee did. My mother. My insurance guy." Liz closed her eyes and raised her head, thinking. She shrugged and looked over at Renee. "I think that's about it."

"Do you think your mom told anyone? Did she mention that to you? Or is there anyone she might have told? Any sisters, brothers, cousins, boyfriends?"

"No. Mom's widowed, no boyfriend. I've got a sister, but I haven't talked to her since Steve's funeral." By way of explaining, Liz added, "She's not a real sweetheart, my sister."

"What's her name?"

"Monica. Monica Sutton. She works at the pier at the other end of the beach. At least she did last I knew."

"Are you seeing anyone now? Did you mention it to the gardener, your hairdresser, the checkout lady at the supermarket?"

Liz chuckled lightly. "Well, you're definitely thorough. No, no boyfriend at the moment. And no, I haven't spilled the beans to any peripheral person. That's just asking for trouble. Next thing you know, the cleaning woman's son will need an operation, you know?"

Graciano nodded, apparently satisfied. He faced Renee and adopted a more gentle tone from the last time he yanked her across the room and lectured her. "Did you tell anyone, any friends, anyone at work, your mother even?"

Renee appreciated his effort to lessen the tension between them. "No, that's Liz's business. I don't gossip," she said adopting his friendly manner.

Graciano addressed Hanif, who had begun eating, and up to this moment hadn't said a word. "When did you find out about the money?"

Hanif kept chewing. "I don't know what you're talking about."

Both detectives immediately turned their attention to Hanif. Renee knew they probably had heard that classic denial about a thousand times in their careers, and it would immediately heighten their suspicion.

"Really?" Grace Slikowksi said. "You have no idea what we're talking about, or why we're here?"

"No, none." Hanif took a huge gulp of iced tea.

Renee felt it necessary to jump in. "Hanif just got into town and—"

"And he was arrested and in court this morning, if I'm not mistaken," Detective Graciano said. "When did you get into town, Hanif?"

"This morning like she said." Hanif gave Renee an anxious look that nobody in the room could possibly miss. Renee groaned to herself. She should have seen this coming.

"Why don't we go downtown to the station where we'll be more comfortable?" Detective Graciano said, still feigning a pleasant attitude.

Hanif choked out a nervous little laugh. "Downtown?"

"I've got a few more questions I'd like to ask you." Graciano flipped his pad closed with a finality that prompted Renee to speak up again.

"You don't have to go anywhere with him," she told Hanif. She faced Detective Graciano squarely, preparing for a fight. "He's comfortable right here, Detective." She tried to keep her tone friendly, but knew this was going to go downhill fast. "He can ask his questions right here if he wants to, Hanif," she said, never taking her eyes off Anthony's face. "But you don't have to answer anything."

Anthony's fake little smile had turned into an icy glare, but Renee didn't back down. The cozy-friendly talk was definitely off the table.

"Don't pick on him because you don't like him," she admonished. "Yeah, I just met him this morning. He's from Iran, and he's going to be a student here. He's staying with me until his sponsor gets back from vacation. He doesn't have any money, no computers hiding in his underwear. He's wearing my husband's old clothes, for heaven's sake."

Anthony glanced at her naked ring finger. "Husband? You're married?" A frown darkened his face for a brief moment before he cleared his throat and quickly continued, his voice crisp and cool. "Did you tell your husband about the check, Mrs. Rose?"

"My ex-husband's clothes. Honestly,"—*Yeah, get the word honestly in there, by all means.* "Hanif's not a suspect in this, and you know it. And I want you to leave him alone." Without really being conscious of it, Renee had placed herself between Hanif and the detectives.

"Cupcake, everybody is a suspect until we get this figured out. He mysteriously shows up right around the time this all starts happening and worms his way into your place. Your best friend is being shaken down, and you've brought him right into her house. That's a little convenient, isn't it?" By the time he finished he was almost shouting.

Renee did not feel intimidated. She worked with lawyers and cops all the time. She would let him get away with the cupcake thing for now. Moving right up into his face, she spoke each word clearly and slowly. "He's with me. When you get the times that those e-mails were sent, you'll see he has an alibi. He was in the holding cell this afternoon and with me tonight."

"And where was he last night?"

They both turned to look at Hanif. "I was at home last night," Hanif said.

"What is the address? Who can I call to verify that?" Anthony flipped open that annoying pad again.

Renee knew that Hanif didn't have a telephone out in the desert. She didn't know how to contact the student exchange people. His passport was back at her place. With Mom out of town, Hanif wasn't going to be able to verify anything easily, and that all looked bad.

"Detective, is this man under arrest?"

Anthony speared her with a look that made her mentally stumble back half a step, but physically, she held her ground. "No, he's not under arrest," he said, his lips tight. "He's just a person of interest at this point, and I am just conducting an investigation of a crime that is being perpetrated against your friend. Your best friend. Remember her?"

Ouch. Renee would not rise to the hit. She stayed on course. "Then he can refuse to answer any of your questions. And if you don't stop badgering him, I'm going to call a lawyer who will make you stop badgering him."

Liz and Detective Slikowski observed this exchange from across the room, keeping an apparent but silent watch on their respective friends. Hanif didn't open his mouth.

"You're impeding the law here," Anthony said. "I could arrest you for that."

"Oh, my ass," Renee fired back. "I'm just telling this innocent man what his options are. And he does not have to answer your questions. This is not Russia. The common person does not have to endure what you cops like to call a civilian encounter. Now if you have some evidence or even probable cause, bring it out so we can find a lawyer and invoke his rights. Otherwise, back off and let us enjoy our cold fried rice."

Each stood their ground, glaring at the other. Renee had her hands on her hips. Her stance firm, her head held high. She may have blinked, but she didn't think so.

"Don't leave the area, sir," Anthony said, his eyes never leaving Renee's face. He snapped his pad shut one last time, turned on his heel, and stomped out. Detective Slikowski thanked Liz and followed, gently closing the door.

"Wow, you were great," Liz said, staring where Detective Graciano had just stood. "I think there's still some testosterone snapping in the air over there."

"And that completes the entertainment portion of our presentation." Renee flopped in the nearest chair exhausted, relieved it was over. Her face felt flushed and her heart pounded. Confrontation was not her favorite thing in life, but she could stand up to a bully when she had to. She had before. She had had to learn how. Although, she had to admit, the detective wasn't all that much of a challenge.

A bully was her father, stinking of vodka, throwing all of her things out of her room and into the backyard grill because she didn't get straight A's. A bully was a husband telling his wife to use the car in the driveway and drive her shivering, vomiting 104-degree temperatured self to the hospital.

The detective was just doing his job. It wasn't personal.

"He doesn't like Hanif, and I don't like him picking on him," Renee finally said.

"Why didn't Hanif stand up for Hanif? What's going on?" Liz asked.

"Okay, it's a little weird what happened, but— first I need a drink."

Liz pulled three beers out of the fridge and passed them around. "I love weird," she said. "I can handle weird. In our line of work next to strange, distorted, bizarre or freakish, weird is good." She settled in a chair, tucked her legs underneath, and reached for the container of noodles.

"I thought Iranians didn't drink alcohol?" Renee watched Hanif take little sips and make faces at the bottle.

"We don't. I have never tasted alcohol before." He wrinkled his nose in distaste. "I was not missing much."

"Well, that's the best Milwaukee has to offer. Sorry." Liz took the bottle away from him. "Besides, you're probably too young."

Renee took a long pull on her beer. Although cold, it went down with a burn. "This all better work out, Hanif, or I just might get charged with obstruction of justice."

She was kidding.

Sort of.

She could think of nothing worse than being handcuffed by Detective Anthony Graciano.

Well, at least in a criminal way.

Chapter 11

Criminal Profiling for Dummies

"Pull over and let me drive, you're going to get us killed," Grace said, clutching the seat belt strap with her left hand and bracing against the dashboard with her right.

"That woman makes me crazy." Anthony swerved to avoid a sport utility vehicle with two surfboards on top.

"You started out crazy, so it was a short trip," Grace said through gritted teeth. "You headed home or what?"

"No, back to the office. We've got to send someone out to check out the e-mail origination point, and I want to have the mother and the sister questioned."

"Tonight?" Grace raised her eyebrows in surprise. "And just who are we going to use for all this work? Boy Scouts? You know half the department is on vacation or out sick. We're so short, I was thinking of knocking over a bank myself."

Anthony suddenly took a sharp right. "This is a one-way street," Grace said, looking around helplessly. "Didn't you see the sign?"

"I saw the sign," he muttered. "You know the old axiom—I'm only going one way." He glanced over at Grace. "Don't hold that handle so hard, you'll break it." He made another sharp turn and placed them on the main drag to the beach/marina area. "There, happy?"

"Happier. Not happy, but happier." She massaged the hand that had had a death grip on the door.

"Lighten up, Slicky. You're making me nervous."

Grace looked at him incredulously. "I'm making you nervous?"

"We're the cops. We can do this. We're on the job."

"Not twenty-four hours a day we're not," she complained.

"Oh, hell, a little overtime never hurt anyone," Anthony said. "Besides you love that office. The flickering lights, the smell of sweat, the ripped furniture. You can't get enough."

Grace studied him for a moment. "You really care about this woman, don't you? I mean, besides your normal preoccupation with saving women victims, which I, for one, really think is sweet." She made a little-girl face and blew him a kiss.

Anthony knew that Grace knew the real story behind his preoccupation with women victims. His last clear memory of his father was of a man hunched over the desk in the den, furiously working the adding machine as though it angered him. The retirement fund, the family savings, all their future plans were gone, taken by a con man who had worked over Anthony's mother. The day his father slammed the front door hard enough to break it from its hinges, got into the family car and never returned, was the day Anthony turned fourteen. His sister fell into gang behavior and quickly went from juvenile hall to state prison. Helpless, he watched his family circle the drain.

Looking at life from the bottom of his mother's gin bottle, he still managed to grow up and hold onto a mostly positive, somewhat skeptical, only slightly skewed view of life. Unable to protect either female in the household had ultimately led to his career choice. Maybe he would have liked to become a pilot or a pro ball player, but he never felt he had the choice. When he graduated from the police academy, he worked especially hard on cases involving jerks that preyed on women and pulled families apart.

"I don't give a tinker's ass about her," Anthony said, screeching to a halt at a red light. He looked over at Grace, trying to keep his face blank.

"Nice try, no buy. When's the last time you had a serious girlfriend, huh?" She screwed her face up in thought. "I can't remember back that far."

"You fixed me up with that school crossing guard last year." Anthony turned to face his partner. "Look how well that turned out."

"You pulled a gun on her," Grace said, exasperated. "She still won't talk to me."

"That whole thing was a misunderstanding. Never mind her, what about that crime scene tech? What's her name?" Anthony stared blankly ahead, willing the woman's name to come.

"Wilma."

"Wilma, right. Total screwball."

"Wilma is a very nice person. She volunteers at the senior center. She grows roses. You dumped her, remember?"

"Yeah, well, I didn't like the way she looked at me."

Grace shifted sideways in her seat. "And just how did she look at you?"

"Like I was the last helicopter leaving Saigon."

"This is a seriously long light." Grace glanced down at her watch. "Really, when was the last time you had a real girlfriend?"

"Define real."

Grace didn't seem to find that funny. "Well?"

"I thought that was a rhetorical question. Look,

I've got women knocking at my door all the time."

"Yeah, but they come in pairs and they're trying to give you religious material."

"Ha-ha. You're a scream."

"Anthony, you're good looking, single, you own your own home. Do you see where I'm going with this?"

"Grace, you're very subtle but, yes, I can follow you."

"Light's green."

Anthony punched the gas and the car lurched forward in a satisfying—to him anyway—jolt.

"Why did she have to act so uppity?" he said pursing his lips, wrinkling his nose, and jiggling his head in his imitation of an up-tight, snobby woman. "She looked at me as if I'd just dropped out of the backside of a dog."

"You questioned her integrity. Was her response less gracious than you think you deserved?"

"Listen, all I care about is this crud ball taking advantage of women. And I do think he's involved somehow. I don't believe in coincidence any more than you do."

Anthony slowed for a stop sign, craned his neck left and right, and sped across the intersection.

"I should give you a ticket for that," Grace admonished, shaking her finger at him. Grace rigidly obeyed all traffic laws in an effort to atone for her partner's frequent and multiple sins.

"He's such a piece of mangy crap," he mumbled out of the side of his mouth.

"A crud ball piece of mangy crap, huh? Where'd you get that from, Criminal Profiling for Dummies?"

Anthony gave a careless shrug of his shoulders. "Saw it on *Cops* once."

"It's not against the law to have a foreign name and be what you'd call exotic," Grace said. "At least not the last I checked." She fiddled with her seat belt where it hit her shoulder "Do you realize you called her Cupcake? I'm surprised she didn't take your head off."

Anthony grimaced. It had not been his best moment. He tried to act nonchalant. "I play by my own rules."

"Oh, yeah? Can I get a copy of those? I don't think I have a complete set." Grace tapped the dashboard frantically. "Watch out for that guy on the bike."

"Oh, hell, I see him," Anthony grumbled. He eased off the gas in deference to his partner's rapidly impending stroke.

"You're such a bad liar. You'd think a guy who dealt with criminals all day could get himself a better act."

He wasn't about to admit it to Grace out loud. If he did, she'd be on him for his clothes, his manners, and probably things he hadn't even thought about yet. She'd want details. He wasn't ready for all that. He could hardly admit it to himself, but he cared very much if Renee got taken. And it wasn't just from the job point of view, although that was important. He was seriously contemplating getting involved with her on a personal level. If she would let him. She would be such a pain in the ass as a girlfriend. A definite complication in his life. He didn't like it, but he didn't know how to stop it, either. Maybe he didn't want to stop it. It was almost out of his control anyway. It would be like trying to stop a falling elevator while he was plunging to his death.

He had to get Grace off his back for now. She wouldn't encourage him to pursue a civilian in an open case, so he decided to give her a little tidbit to chew on. That would give him some time to get a grip on his feelings for Renee without Grace's interference. "All right, you know who I think is pretty hot? That Liz Sutton," He waggled his eyebrows for effect.

Grace just stared at him. Was the eyebrow waggling thing too much?

"You like Liz Sutton? I guess that computes. You hardly said two words to her, you old charmer you."

Grace dug her cell phone out of her pocket and answered a personal call. Anthony was out of the hot seat for now. Renee Rose. He irritated the woman just by breathing. He had thought all night about ways to get around that. Maybe he'd have to bring out the charm. It had been a very long time since he'd used charm. He was a bit rusty. More than a bit. Usually, just his badge worked on impressing women, but this one found cops annoying. He had done a computer search of her, all in the line of duty, of course, and found out that she had been married to a cop. She knew the law well enough not to be intimidated by whatever came out of his mouth. She certainly didn't like being told what was good for her.

When he researched the ex-husband, he found that the guy had had a reputation as a bad dude and somewhat of an asshole, so unless she was a slow learner, she definitely didn't want to get involved with that same kind of guy again; someone bossy, intimidating, who ordered her around. Anthony cringed. That's all he'd been doing with Renee from the moment he met her. Anthony vowed to stop acting like an angry maniac and start being calmer, sweeter. Whatever type of guy she liked, he would become that. *Listen to me*, he groaned inwardly. He was stepping off the deep end with a big, stupid grin on his face.

He sure hoped Renee wasn't interested in that young guy she was helping. He was exotic, Grace had said. Anthony thought he looked a little girlie with his long, swishy hair. What kind of man wears his hair like that? The total opposite of her ex-husband, which, in itself, worried Anthony. When the creep looked over and gave Renee that pitiful look, Anthony had wanted to smash his face. Oh yeah, he was definitely using Renee. Anthony clenched his fists around the steering wheel. The thought of punching him and breaking those teeth sent a shiver of revulsion through him. Not very good cop behavior, but his desire to protect Renee had become overwhelming, almost primal. He had to get it under control. This guy was probably a small-time con. But what if he wasn't small time? She could get hurt, robbed, car stolen, knocked on the head—that stupid, foolish, irritating, wonderful, pulse-quickening woman.

Grace's voice broke into his thoughts. "Why don't you pull into that little store up ahead and get us some coffee. I'll boot up the in-car computer and see if I can get information on the mother and the sister. There's no one at the office that can help us anyway. It would be a wasted trip." She pulled the computer tray around to her side of the car and started working the keys.

Anthony backed into a slot that said No Parking.

Grace raised her eyebrows at him.

"What? That sign? They don't mean me." He pointed his thumb to his chest. "I buy my losing Lottery tickets at this place every week. They love me here. I'll be right back." Anthony jumped out of the car and slammed the door. As he jogged up to the store entrance, he yelled back, "Hey, watch out for bad guys, this is a crappy neighborhood."

Through the store window, Anthony could see his partner working the keyboard, entering the details on the individuals they were looking for. The system was still in search mode when Anthony got back in the car with two cups.

Grace opened her lid and made a face. "You'd think a man with a gun could get better coffee," she complained. "Here, you drink this, I can't."

Anthony dumped both drinks out the window and tossed the cups into the back seat onto the pile of junk that had accumulated there over the last few weeks. Months maybe.

"I have to clean out this car," he muttered. A few blissful moments of silence passed as Grace worked the laptop, narrowing the defining information. "Grace, are my clothes bad?"

Grace laughed right out loud. "Man, you have got it bad for her, don't you?"

Anthony waved a dismissing hand at her. "A guy can't be concerned about his looks without getting comments?"

"Since when do you care about your looks?"

"Since someone, and yes it happened to be Ms. Rose, pointed out that my ties were so hideous she couldn't even concentrate. She was probably just being rude."

Anthony watched Grace's fingers fly. She was as good, or better, than he when it came to finagling information out of that box of circuits and tiny green lights.

"She was being rude all right, but she's right. And she's not the first person to ever point that out to you."

"You don't count."

"Why the hell not?" Grace said, turning away from the glowing screen, "I have to see you every day."

"Well, maybe if my clothes are that bad, you should stop in every morning and organize my closet for me," he retorted. "I wouldn't want to offend your senses."

"I know you're being a smartass, but that's not a bad idea. I could hang some matching things together."

Anthony snorted.

After a moment, Grace said, "I always thought you were color blind. Did you know that?"

Crap, it was that bad. He had never given wardrobe much thought. His priority had been catching the bad guys. He got up at two cracks before dawn, took a shower, and threw on whatever he grabbed in the dark. *See how that woman is complicating your life already? She's trouble, no doubt about it.*

Grace tapped the screen. "Here, I found the mother's and sister's current addresses. It's not too late, we can swing by them both tonight." Grace continued to play around the keyboard. "We should question the insurance guy, too."

Anthony pulled out of the parking lot and headed toward the south marina, the sleazy end of the beach district, toward the sister's place. He glanced down at the address Grace had written for him.

"I think this is that old pink motel on the corner by the liquor store. You know the one with the broken sign that doesn't even blink any more, it just gives off a zzzzt sound?"

"I think you're right." Grace kept an obvious eye on the traffic, which was thankfully light at this time of night. "You know, that insurance money Liz Sutton just received, that hundred grand? I'm not saying it's not a nice chunk of change, but if you think about it, it's only about a year's salary for a court reporter. But the sister, on the other hand..." Grace let it hang.

"That's a lot of money for someone who lives in a fifty-dollar-a-week motel," Anthony finished the thought.

"Sure is."

"Although, the demand only asked for fifty

grand. That is odd. Why wouldn't they go for the full amount?"

"It's a loose end. I hate loose ends. Let's just see if sis is home."

Chapter 12

The Finer Points of Revenge

Monica placed the straw to her nose, bent her head over the nightstand, and inhaled a fat line of cocaine. She straightened then sniffed in sharply a few times before rubbing some white powder on her gums with her finger.

"This is good stuff," she murmured as she flopped back on her bed to savor the moment. She idly played with the fraying fringe on the worn bedspread and stared at the brown stains on the ceiling. One of them looked like a dog taking a drink. Her two companions were sitting at the wobbly dining table drinking coffee. "Don't you guys want some?" she asked, keeping an eye on the dog.

"I can't do that every day," Dante said. "Gives me a headache." Although Dante had been in the United States for fifteen years, he still carried a slight Puerto Rican accent. He had dark skin, dark eyes and dark intentions. Monica knew enough to be wary of him but at times he proved useful.

"I'll take a hit," the second male said, putting his Styrofoam coffee cup down and moving toward the drug.

"Too much of that stuff will rot your brains, Dirt," Dante warned. "What you got left anyway."

The skinny man's real name was Roger, but a short career as a gravedigger left him with the nickname. His clothes hung on his scrawny frame and his face was pale and puffy. He looked ready for a body bag himself.

"Yeah, well, I'll tell you when I've had too much," Dirt retorted, appearing agitated at being lectured, and bravely firing back. He used the razor blade to chop up some white chunks, then formed a thin line.

"You won't be able to," Dante replied. "You'll be too far gone to even know." Dante tipped his head back and sniffed loudly. Monica knew why he was so stuffed up. She had treated last night because she wanted a big favor from him.

"You still all blocked up?"

He tried to inhale quickly and winced from the strain. He began to gingerly rub the side of his nose.

"And I'll tell you something else, dude," Dante said. "We're not going out on the yacht again with you all messed up. You didn't tie her up properly in Cayman, we nearly went adrift."

"I caught it right off." Dirt dismissed his boss with a wave. He inhaled the powder using a rolled up dollar bill.

"No, no, amigo. No more going out messed up or Mr. Sinclair will leave our butts on a foreign pier somewhere."

Dirt looked over to where Dante was seated. "I feel really bad for your mom, you know? Like her furniture and stuff."

Dante raised his eyebrows. "What are you talking about?"

"Well, her chairs must all be ruined, what with that big stick up your ass." Dirt howled with laughter, exposing badly stained teeth. He fell across the unoccupied bed holding his stomach.

Dante's face turned dark. He fingered the large mole on his chin. "It must be the drugs making you brave, dude."

Dirt wiped his runny nose on his arm. "With that big stick up your ass," he repeated, rolling around, trying to catch his breath.

"Guys, save the hilarity for another time," Monica said, sensing Dante's irritation and wanting to avoid trouble in her room. The manager wasn't real happy with her as it was. She sat up and blinked a few times. The drug began to make her mind sparkle, and she was ready to tackle the problem. "I was glad to see you two are in dry dock for a couple weeks. I have some work for you." Monica flipped Detective Graciano's card at Dante. Dante made a grab at it as it flew by his head.

"First, though, I don't like the cops at my door."

"There's no trouble. Only in your mind." Dante glanced down at the business card with the JPD logo on it. "You don't even know what this is about."

"And what if it's about Steve, huh? What about that?"

"It's been a year. He ain't here to ask about Steve. Relax. We took care of Stevey-boy. He ain't gonna make an appearance, okay?" Dante took a huge gulp of his coffee. "This stuff is cold," he complained. He threw the cup toward the wastebasket and missed. Dribbles of coffee soaked into the shabby rug.

"Well, I don't want to talk to no cop about nothing." Monica, unconcerned about the carpet, sat forward, reached deeply down the back of the waistband of her skirt, and scratched vigorously.

"Last time I saw Steve, he was bobbing in the water seven miles out at sea," Dante assured her.

"Yeah, but you don't know if he was dead," Dirt said, always the thorn, never the rose. He gestured toward Monica, waving his arms wildly. "The sea was so rough out there, man, we was scairt the boat was gonna swamp. Man, it was only a little 45-footer. We shot at him a couple times, but he kept bouncing around on the waves, so we just left him."

"I hit him, I told you that a hundred times." Dante's expression turned sharp. Monica watched the emotions play over his face. The effort to stay seated and not punch Dirt in his boney head seven or eight times became obvious by his body language. "He was face down in the water, wasn't he? I ain't gonna go over this again. Steve's gone. End of story." He faced Monica. "I don't know what that cop wants, but it ain't about Steve," he said with finality. "Enough with this bull. You said something about a good job. What's up?"

Dirt fingered the scar on his cheek, a souvenir from a direct hit with a whiskey bottle. "One more line first," he said, awkwardly rolling to the side of the bed the drugs were on.

Dante quickly moved in between Dirt and the white powder. "Enough, man. No more. I need you sharp now."

Dirt stood and faced Dante nose-to-nose. Dante's right eye twitched slightly, and his mouth hardened into a thin line.

"This would make me sharp," Dirt whined.

"Yeah, you're a tack right now."

Dirt plopped on the bed in a disappointed heap. Everyone knew Dante ran the show.

"So, what'd you need?" Dante asked, turning toward Monica, who had watched the last exchange between the two men with barely concealed boredom. Dirt seriously needed to get some balls.

"That jerk wad Richard is what I called you here for. I had a plan going, a little scam, to get fifty grand out of my sister." Dirt whistled at the amount. "She don't need it and I do, so I had a deal going, and I let Richard in on it."

"That bum is a moron. What are you doing with him?" Dante wrinkled his nose and shook his head then gave Monica a quick head-to-toe once over.

"Never mind. You two were meant for each other."

"I loved the guy, okay?" Monica flung back. Her face pinched as a surprise sting of tears hit. She shook it off. This was no time to get mushy over some bum who left her in the rain. Or out in the lurch. Or whatever the hell that expression was.

"You sure sis has that kind of money?" Dante asked. Monica wiped her eyes, knowing he was unmoved by tears and indifferent to the concept of loving someone.

"Oh, yeah," she sniggered.

"What's so funny?"

"It's Steve's life insurance check. I saw the letter the insurance company sent to the marina closing out the case and releasing his boat for sale."

"Now ain't that something? Ole Steve may make us some money after all," Dirt said.

"Richard took off with my computer and I need that laptop to make this thing work," Monica said, ignoring Dirt and addressing Dante. You didn't have to be a weatherman to know which way the wind was blowing.

"I been collecting information on Liz. I got it all right here in this journal." She tapped a ragged blue notebook. "I got her e-mail, all her phone numbers, her friend's info, all that stuff in case I need a number or something fast." She tossed him a photo of two young girls. "This was me and Liz."

Monica quickly outlined the plan, smiling inwardly, because she had Dante's full attention, and that didn't happen often.

"You two look nothing alike," he said, holding the photo up and comparing it to Monica. "She's pretty. What happened? You got adopted or something?"

"Funny man. Pay attention. It all hangs on Liz getting these e-mails. The guy I stole the computer from is traveling on business right now, but sooner or later, he'll get home and cancel his service. I ain't got a lot of time to get this done."

"We can't use another computer?" Dante asked.

"I don't know crap about computers. I only know I got the code to get into that laptop and that e-mail account. I pretended like I was real interested and told this guy at the airport how smart he was and rubbed his leg a few times and the dumb bugger showed me everything right there in the coffee shop."

Monica dragged herself off the bed and went into the bathroom to try to blow her nose. "I know Richard sent at least two e-mails out, cuz I helped him with them." She rummaged around the small room for a moment, then poked her head out. She gestured a toilet paper-clenched fist toward the front door. "I went out and looked around for him a couple times, this morning even, but I don't know where he went."

"That's amazing," Dante said, shaking his head.

"What? That Richard would do this?"

"No, that you got out of bed in the morning."

"Ha-ha. You suck," Monica said, knowing she could get away with a lot of things that Dirt couldn't.

"Maybe he just pawned the computer for drug money," Dirt suggested. "That's what I'd do."

"And that's why you're never in charge," Dante said.

Dirt made a face and flopped on his back. "Hey, that looks like a dog up there," he said, pointing to the ceiling.

"What makes you think he's still around," Dante asked.

"I know this bum, been sleeping with him for a year. He ain't crazy about Florida, but he knows the beach, the bars, all the places. He's comfortable here. He don't have no money. He's on foot around here somewhere."

"Smart thing to do would be to hitchhike out of here," Dante offered.

"Lucky for us he's not too bright then, huh? I checked the two local pawn shops and no one's been in with a laptop in the last two days. He's got it, he's around, and he's gonna try to run this scam by himself. I'd bet my last breath on it."

"So what do you want us to do?" Dante said.

"Find him and get my computer back. It'll have all the messages he's sent. Then we'll know where we are in this scam."

"And if we find him, what do we do with him?"

"I'll leave that part up to you. You're better at that stuff. I don't want him around knowing what the deal is. He could screw it up just for spite."

"Understood," Dante said, a wicked grin crossing his face. "We'll take care of him. Now, what's in it for us?"

"You'll be my new partners, of course. Fifty-fifty. We'll get the dough, blow this town, and you can get off working on that yacht like you were some kind of slave for that fat, old, white guy." Monica enjoyed the look on Dante's face. She instinctively knew how to touch a sore spot. It was like a talent with her. "Richard would never even think that I'd come after him. He thinks he's safe, so he won't be careful. I tell you, I know this guy."

"You got a picture? I sort of remember him. Tall, skinny, blonde hair?" Dante asked.

Monica pulled a photo out of the nightstand drawer. It was of her and Richard at the air show on the beach last year. "He's a little skinnier now," Monica commented as she wiped the picture with her finger. It wasn't a good shot of her. "I look like crap," she complained, handing the photo over to Dante.

"We'll find him," Dante promised, studying the happy couple in his hand.

"He won't know what hit him," Dirt added, apparently unable to grasp the finer points of revenge.

"I'd prefer it if he did," Monica said.

"Understood," Dante nodded. "I'll make sure he knows. Steve was ours first. It's only right we get him back."

Chapter 13

The Italian Job

"So, tell me about yourself, Hanif." Liz pushed some of last night's chicken fried rice around on her plate. "With all that went on I didn't get the story."

Renee and Hanif had ended up staying the night. It all started when Liz brought a pitcher of lemonade out to her back porch and showed him the pool. The screened-in area was terraced, and covered with fragrant tropical plants. The multi-level pool sported a small waterfall—a true oasis by anyone's description. When Liz flipped on the lights, and he saw the water, it was as though he had seen a dinosaur. His mouth dropped open, and his eyes got huge.

"I have imagined such a thing in my dreams," he said. "It is—" he faltered, his lips trembled slightly.

"Pretty?" Liz said.

"Beautiful?" Renee offered.

"Taking the breath away," he said almost in a whisper. He touched two fingertips to his forehead, his mouth, and his heart, then did a little bow. "I am blessed for having this experience. I am thankful. Allah, be praised."

Kneeling at the edge, he dipped his hand. "So clear. So cool." Making little swirls, he asked, "What is that smell?"

"That's called chlorine and it keeps the water

clean. That water is not for drinking though."

"Not for drinking? What is the purpose then?"

"We swim in it."

"You mean this water is only for—what do you call it? For playing? Um, for recreational time?" Hanif's eyes were shiny with amazement.

"That's right."

"You have so much water that you put some aside just for the pleasure of it." He slowly shook his head at the wonder of that statement.

Hanif stood, tipped his head back, closed his eyes and held his face up. He raised his arms and made little circles with them.

"What are you doing?" Renee asked.

"This is moisture," he said with glee in his voice. "There's moisture all around me." He opened his eyes and began to do a little wobbly jig on the deck. He stopped and abruptly turned to face her.

"Is it permissible for me to sit here and enjoy the moisture for a while?"

That was the first time Renee had ever heard anyone say they wanted to enjoy Florida's moisture. She wondered how he felt about mosquitoes.

"You can do more than just look at it, you can go in it if you'd like," Liz said.

Hanif almost fell over in a faint. "Get in? Me? I can step into your water?" He looked down at his clothes. "What about—"

Liz stopped him. "I must have some old shorts around. Let me go find something."

Renee watched her hurry into the house and rummage around in the hall closet. Apparently finding the box she wanted, she dumped the contents on the floor and spread them around. "This is gonna be so fun." She snatched up a pair of cut-off jeans. "These will work."

"How did you bathe back home with no water?" Renee asked.

"We cleanse ourselves with sand," Hanif said.

"Ouch. Sand? Really?"

"It is so hot that we do not have a problem with—how do you say? Perspire?"

"Perspiration. Sweat."

"Yes, sweat. The moisture evaporates off of our bodies and does not soil our garments. If we need to clean our hands or feet, we rub them in the sand."

"So essentially you sandpaper yourself clean." Renee thought a moment. "I could make a fortune selling hand cream over there." She leaned over in her chair and peered down the hall. "You coming?" she yelled to Liz. "I got a great new business idea here."

"Hold on, I'm getting my camera," Liz said. The muffled voice told Renee that Liz was now in her bedroom closet.

"We also use our right hand for eating and doing clean work, and our left hand for unclean activities," Hanif explained.

"Oh, I've read about that." Renee tipped her head back to coax the ice out of her glass. "That's why a thief will have his right hand cut off as a punishment, right?"

"Yes, that way a thief can be identified but also he has to lead a life of using his unclean hand to eat." Hanif shook his head. "A very undesirable state to be in."

Once Hanif changed and actually got in the water, the women couldn't get him out. Hours went by while he played, splashed, and floated. Renee made another pitcher of lemonade, spiked this time, and watched Liz try to teach Hanif how to swim. When he finally got out of the pool, all wrinkly and shivering, it was after midnight. Renee had had too much to drink and drive so they decided to spend the night in Liz's guest room.

"All right, before the interrogation begins,"

Renee interjected, sipping on her coffee, "let me set the record straight. Yes, he's the guy from court yesterday. No, he's not a love interest."

Liz turned a wry smile on her friend. "And what about the cute detective?"

"What about him? He makes my skin crawl. He makes me sick. I can't stand him."

"Uh-huh, just what I thought. You're crazy about him."

Renee made gagging noises over the side of her chair.

"Very mature. Oh, stop denying it. Look, for once, let down your guard. Let down your hair. Let down your mother." She waggled her fork at her best friend. "It'll do you some good."

"I can't. I'm afraid. He's a cop." Renee said the word *cop* like her mother said the words *blow job*, with exaggerated emphasis and a squinched up face. Renee didn't take sex lightly, and the detective wasn't the kind of man she would have chosen for a serious relationship.

"What if I get involved and he disappears faster than cupcakes at a pot party?"

Hanif, who had been sampling all the different Chinese dishes, had been quiet up to this point. "I agree."

"What would you know about any of this? And who asked you anyway? What are you, nineteen?" Renee said, the line of conversation making her cranky. She wasn't exactly chumming the oceans for men, but that was her business. Her failure with men wasn't legendary. But it was close.

"It's just a universal standard that applies to all cultures. The human being needs to remain social. Once that phenomena stops you might as well lay down and wait for Al-Lah," Hanif said.

"Wow, he's pretty deep," Liz said.

"You learned a lot of big words in that little

tent," Renee said, annoyed that he agreed with Liz. She ignored him and turned to her friend.

"Okay, here's the deal about Hanif here. He's mom's foreign exchange student this year. Last minute, he had to travel earlier than planned. Mom is on her Christmas cruise with the girls this week, so I told her he could stay with me."

"Why was he arrested?"

"He was waiting on the beach for me to get home. They thought he was a vagrant. I should have picked him up at the airport, but with all this Steve drama, it just slipped my mind."

Hanif gave a piece of chicken to Beans, who looked at him with adoring eyes.

"Don't feed her too much, or she'll get the poops," Liz said.

He quickly withdrew his outstretched hand. "Poops?"

"You don't want to know, trust me."

Liz sat back in her chair. Wiping her mouth with a napkin, she studied Hanif. He made funny faces at the dog while Beans, thrilled to have so much play time, twirled around in little circles. Liz cut her eyes to Renee and said matter-of-factly, "So, you're babysitting."

"Yep, that's about the scoop."

****

The knock wasn't friendly. That should have tipped them off. Liz was in the process of tossing Beans' food and favorite toy in a duffle bag, packing to stay a few nights at Renee's.

She smiled as she went to the entry door window and pulled back the curtain. "Maybe I got a package." She abruptly let the curtain drop. "Oh, crap."

"What's the matter," Renee asked through the pass-through to the kitchen where she had been washing dishes.

Liz turned and frowned. "It's my sister."

"Monica? Really?" Renee wiped her hands and came to the front door and peeked out. "Yep, that's her."

Liz looked like she was considering whether to answer the door or not.

"If I don't open the door, the neighbors might be subjected to a dramatic scene."

Renee knew from experience that Monica could make a dandy of a scene. "I could go wait in the bedroom if you want."

"No, stay here. She doesn't like you, maybe it'll make her leave faster." Liz scowled as she tapped in the security code and swung open the door. "Monica? What are you doing here? I thought you were in South America or something."

"Why would you think that?" Monica shouldered her way past Liz and into the cool interior of the house. The scent of dime-store makeup and three-dollar vodka was so strong Renee could smell it from where she was seated on a barstool at the breakfast nook. Beans retreated under the dining room table, a low growl humming in her throat.

"Maybe because that's what you said at Steve's funeral," offered Liz, closing the door with a reluctant nudge of her shoulder.

"Steve's funeral?" Monica looked surprised, then genuinely perplexed. Her face lit up. "Oh, I remember. What I said was I was banging a guy from Peru."

"Sorry. Can't keep up with you,"

Monica spotted Renee and her face fell. "Oh, hi."

"Monica," Renee said. No sense telling the woman it was nice to see her.

"Still got that scrawny mutt, huh?" Monica bent slightly and peered under the table.

Liz cut her eyes in Renee's direction on the mutt comment. Renee knew there were so many buttons

Monica could choose, Liz was going to have problems keeping her cool. The two sisters had grown up in the same house, went to the same schools, were loved by the same parents. It was impossible to pinpoint when they started to grow apart into the two drastically dissimilar females standing in that room.

"Why are you here? You haven't been in contact with me in over a year."

"It's Christmas for crap's sake," Monica said. "Can't a girl visit family at the holidays?"

"I don't recall you coming over last year at Christmas," Liz muttered.

Monica began wandering around the living room, her eyes darting quickly, seemingly appraising the contents. Renee wondered if she would try to steal something right under both their noses.

"Your place looks great, as usual. Must be nice to have a little moola and be able to set yourself up like this."

"I earn my moola," Liz fired back hotly. "You still selling drugs at the dock?" Button number two. Or was that three? Renee had lost count. It was always like this when Monica came around.

"You don't have to be so mean," Monica said, a hurt look playing across her face. That face was fake. Renee was sure of it, and she knew Liz knew it, too. Liz held her ground. Renee gave Monica ten seconds to change her tactic. Monica relaxed, plopped down on the couch, and smiled up at Liz. It had only taken five. "Come on, let's not fight. We live different lifestyles and we're different characters, and that's the way it's been for years. We're like water and sugar."

"That's water and oil. It's sweet as sugar and— never mind." Liz ran a frustrated hand through her hair. "Yeah, we're different. And I don't trust your character. Again, I'll ask you, what are you doing here?"

Renee sincerely hoped Monica wasn't homeless or wanted by the law or something that would involve Liz involuntarily getting tangled up in some huge mess.

"How's mom?" Monica said, not very subtly changing the subject.

"Why don't you go see her and find out?"

"I don't think she'll buzz me through her security gate."

"No, probably not. Not after the last time when you left with her jewelry."

Monica waved her hand in the air. Her nails were dirty and jagged. "I got that all straightened out. She was gonna leave it to me in her will, so I got it a little early. What's the big deal? Anyway, that's early history."

"Ancient history," Liz said through clenched teeth. Renee remembered that fiasco. It had been six months ago, but maybe that was a lifetime to Monica.

"So, whatcha doing?" Monica began fumbling around in her purse.

Liz gazed toward Renee hopelessly. "Don't tell her you're leaving," Renee mouthed. If that little piece of news slipped out, when she came back, her house would be empty. Either that or it would be full of bums crashing for the night.

Monica pulled out a cigarette. "I bet I can't smoke in here, right?"

"I'm getting ready to host a party tonight," Liz lied smoothly. "No, you can't smoke in here."

Monica's eyes lit up and she ran her tongue over her lipsticked mouth. "Party food? New people? You know Richard just left me. I'm kind of down in the dumps about it. I could use a party."

Renee didn't know who Richard was and felt sure Liz didn't care. She wondered how deep this party story would have to go. Liz wasn't good at lying.

" I've got about five hundred things to do, so if you would just come to the point and tell me what you want so I can say no and we can part company, that would be great."

"So who's coming?"

"What's it to you?"

"Just wondering is all." She picked up a paperweight from the side table and examined it. "I don't know why none of your friends don't like me."

"Gee, and you're so adorable. Put that down and cut the crap. What do you want?"

Monica sat forward and put what she probably thought passed for genuine on her face. "Okay, it's just a little thing. I really need to use your computer to check—um—to check my e-mail. I'm waiting for a really important message." As Monica warmed up to her apparently impromptu story, her face became more animated. "I might have a job in Italy and I'm waiting for the okay."

Liz stared at her sister for a moment, speechless. First of all, genuine wasn't a look Monica could pull off and Renee knew Liz wasn't buying it. And secondly, an Italian job? Please. That was one for the books.

Monica forged on. "You don't happen to have a book on speaking Italian, do you?"

"Give me a break, Monica. First off, you don't even have an e-mail account. And you having a job offer from Italy is as realistic as you becoming vice president of a bank."

Monica managed a hurt look. "I do, too. Just let me use the stupid computer for a few minutes, and I'll be out of your way and you can clean and party prep until you puke."

Renee felt confident Liz wasn't about to let Monica on her computer. God only knew what she was up to and what trouble or damage she'd leave when she left.

"The library down the street has free computer access," Liz said.

"Way down there?" Monica whined, inclining her head in the direction of the city center down the road. "It's 100 degrees out today."

"It's only four blocks." Liz pulled her curtains aside and peered out her front window. "There's no car. How did you get here?"

"A friend dropped me, if you must know."

"I don't want to know anything about you. Really. I don't care. You've stepped all over me and mom so many times that you've left nothing for us to care about."

Monica softened her voice. "But it's Christmas, Liz, and—"

"Save it, Monica. Holidays don't mean a thing to you. It's just another day to work up a new scam on someone." Liz opened the front door and folded her arms over her chest. Her face sharp with the effort to look stern, she stated, "You need to leave now. And I'm going to ask you nicely not to come back."

Renee knew it killed her to act this mean to her sister, but if she didn't, Liz would be toast by New Years. There just wasn't any other way to deal with Monica. She was a drug addict and no amount of love and rehab would turn her around. Monica loved the life she led. She often said she would have it no other way. Liz and her mom wanted no part of it. They both had learned the hard way that they either protected themselves or got taken to the cleaners. Renee wasn't worried about Liz's mom right now. She lived in a guarded, gated community called Oak Hills. Ironically, the property contained no oaks and not a single hill. Renee assumed they had all been leveled to construct the buildings. After all, this was Florida. Nevertheless, Monica couldn't get into her mom's place unless she used a SWAT team.

Monica smoothed down her skirt and played with the frayed hem. She tried to tuck her left foot, which had a broken shoe strap that hung at an awkward angle, behind her right foot. After a moment of improvised grooming, she held up two hands, fingers spread. "Look—" she started.

Liz cut her off and adopted a ruthless tone. "Monica, you made your bed a long time ago. Now go lie in it."

Monica jumped up from the couch and glared at her. "Don't I ever get to change the sheets?"

"Not out of my closet, you don't."

Monica stared over at the laptop sitting on Liz's desk. It was only about six feet away. "Don't you even think about it," Liz warned her. "I'll take you down so fast you'll think a car hit you." Tough words. Liz had never hit anyone in her life.

Monica folded like a cheap lawn chair. She gave Liz a steely-eyed, haughty look, turned on her heel, and stomped out the door. Renee could see her through the picture window high stepping down the walk, her shoe strap flapping, right hand extended skyward, middle finger held erect.

"Merry Christmas to you, too." Liz muttered. She began to shake and had to sit down before her knees gave way. "That was awful."

"You handled her well," Renee said, sitting next to her on the couch. She put a warm hand on Liz's knee. "You handled her well," she repeated.

"It's hard watching her hit rock bottom and wallow in it. Even if it's by choice, it's still painful."

"Only Monica can turn her life around."

Liz gave her friend a little smile. "You're singing to the choir, woman."

Beans came out from under the table and jumped into Liz's lap, a warm, little bundle of energy and wet nose. After a few moments, Liz got up and reset the alarm.

"Well, I gotta finish packing."

It wasn't until Liz went to lock up and leave for Renee's that she realized her gold watch, which had been on the end table, was missing.

Chapter 14

Steamed Heat

When Hanif opened Renee's front door, he had a piece of cake in one hand and frosting on his face. "Do you know about this?" he said, jiggling the cake. Crumbs bounced off his shirt and onto the carpeted hallway.

Anthony glanced at the cake a moment, and then fixed his eyes on Hanif. "Are you asking me if I know about cake?"

"This is the best thing I have ever had," Hanif enthused. "Well, maybe not the best. Orange juice is good, too." Hanif took a huge bite and chewed happily, making little grunting noises. He put a hand on the doorjamb and left a chocolate smudge.

"Were you raised in a barn or what?"

Hanif looked confused. He stopped chewing for a moment. "A barn?" he said with a mouthful of cake.

"Nice. Never mind. Is Ms. Rose or Ms. Sutton here?"

"Who?"

Anthony sighed deeply. What a simpleton. He spoke very slowly. "Is either Renee or Liz here?"

"Liz has not arrived yet, and Renee went down to the first floor to someplace called Jim."

Anthony handed Hanif his business card. "Please tell them that I was here and that I'll be back later. I have a few more questions for them."

Anthony started to leave then added, "And don't think for one minute that I'm not watching you."

"Uh, okay," Hanif said. "It is a free country." Hanif raised his eyes in a quizzical look. "It is a free country, right?"

"Look, wiseass." Anthony pointed a finger and came within an inch of Hanif's chest. "I don't think your act is funny, and I'm on to you. If you're involved here, and I'm sure you are, you're going down."

"Down. Sure, okay. Whatever you want," Hanif said amiably. "You want some cake?"

Anthony shook his head in frustration. "No, I don't want any damn cake." What was up with this guy? Maybe there was something mentally wrong with him. Anthony stomped down the hall to the elevator and punched the button.

"Goodbye," Hanif said. Anthony looked back. Hanif stepped out into the hallway, waved his hand, then retreated into the apartment, gently shutting the door.

"That is one strange dude," Anthony muttered.

Grace had the day off and went holiday shopping, so Anthony was working alone today. First thing this morning, he had cleaned out his car, dragging two large garbage bags to the trash can. Then he took a shower and dressed carefully in something he felt certain matched.

Unable to reach Liz's sister last night, he had left his card in the door of the motel room she rented. The lights were on at her listed place of employment, Blue Water Marina, and a quick chat with her boss revealed that he "fired her butt" a few weeks ago for not showing up. The marina owner advised the detectives that Monica hung around with a couple of guys that worked on and off on the large yacht docked at the end of the pier.

Then he and Grace had made a quick trip over

to Liz's mother's condo where they were told by the guard that she was out of town.

He knew he didn't really need to talk to either Liz or Renee today, but he just had to see Renee. He was banging his head against her like a moth on a hot light bulb. He knew he'd probably go up in flames, but he couldn't help himself.

The elevator door opened on the lower level. When he stepped out, he found himself directly in front of two doors that identified the men's and women's gyms. He opened the door that said "Women" a crack and peered in.

"Ms. Rose, are you in here?"

He stepped in a little further, closing his eyes in a polite gesture. He called out her name again. When there was no answer, he opened his eyes. The room was empty, save for the expensive equipment that sat silent. A noise drew his attention to the back of the gym area. He crisscrossed the room between bulky weight equipment and rowing machines. He found a door with a small glass panel at the top and a sign that read, "Spinning Class."

"Ms. Rose," he yelled. Peeking in the panel revealed nothing. Maybe the dickhead had been wrong, or sent him on a wild goose chase for fun. Anthony opened the door. This room was also empty except for four rows of stationery bikes. "Ms. Rose?" He saw something on the bench at the end of the last row of bicycles and headed toward it. It was a pile of clothes; a pair of jeans, some sort of white blouse, and a pair of lace panties with a hot pink bra.

That stopped him. Actually, it stopped his heart. A soft hissing noise drew his attention away from the undies. He edged past the bench like it might be poison and went around the corner. Here the hiss became more distinct, and he realized it was steam. Turning to retreat his gaze fell on a clear, steam-filled cubicle. Dear God, she was in the steam room.

He tried to make his feet work but they were frozen. The cop in him ordered him to move, but the man made him stay.

The light scent of a women's gym mingled with the faint traces of exotic perfumes left behind by their owners. He licked his lips and stared at the mist behind the door. A rivulet of water slowly made its way down the glass, clearing a small, blurry path. He caught movement behind the door, a slight shifting. Every drop of his blood rushed directly to where it wanted to be. She fiddled with her towel, removing it from her body and placing it on the bench behind her. Her backside was to him. And what a backside it was. She turned to sit down and his breathing stopped. He prayed she couldn't see him standing there like a common peeping Tom. He sternly told himself to move at the first opportunity, but right now, it was too late. She was facing him. She would see the movement. She lay down on her back and raised her arms above her head, completely, utterly and unbelievably naked.

His brain shut off. His libido was out of control. Another rivulet cleared a larger spot. His mouth went dry. He couldn't actually see the moisture, but he knew her body would be slick with it. Her breasts rose with each breath, and he found himself breathing along with her rhythm. His gaze traveled where his hands wanted to go. She pulled her hair up and away from her body with one hand and shifted her legs, letting one dangle over the edge of the bench. The small dark patch between her legs almost crippled him.

Dizzy with desire, his erection intense to the point of being painful, his cop side screamed at him to move, to step back. She would be furious if she found out he'd stood here when she had imagined herself alone. And what if someone were to come in? Besides it being obnoxious of him to watch her, it was against the law. He could justify his coming upon her quite by accident, but his standing here this long would be impossible to explain.

She crooked one arm and placed it over her eyes. This was it. The perfect time to leave. He slowly backed out, taking care to not make an iota of sound, even though the hissing of the steam would probably cover it. He nearly tripped when he backed around the corner and into a bike. He righted himself and ran to the exit door. Once outside, he put his back to the wall and slid down in a crouch.

Holy Mother of God. He ran his hand through his hair and let out a frustrated moan. There would be no going back now. If he had been mildly attracted to her before, he was in full blown lust now. He shut his eyes and the image of her lost in clouds of steam filled his head. He knew this image would come to him at night for a long time. It took a few minutes, but his breathing returned to normal. The bulge in his pants? Well, he had no control over that. He looked around to be sure he was alone and was about to adjust himself to ease the strain when he saw the surveillance camera. He had been filmed going into the women's room. Crap. Double crap. Now he'd have to cover by pretending he'd gone into the wrong room. He needed to splash some water on his face anyway, so he quickly got to his feet and headed for the men's room.

Chapter 15

Back From the Grave

Monica had to hike all the way down from the bus stop to her room after her disastrous visit with Liz. The bitch wouldn't let her even look at her computer. Monica lay on her bed, rubbing her sore feet.

"You are so gonna get yours," she said to the ceiling. "Ain't no reason to treat me like that."

Monica's cell phone chirped. She glanced down at the caller ID and took the call.

"What?"

"I didn't hear from you last night," the man said. His voice sounded deep and calm on the surface, but an underlying spark of tension crackled through the line.

"The plan is still the same, only the players have changed."

Monica wasn't afraid of this guy.

"Are you sure you know what you're doing?"

"I'll handle this little setback. It's still on the mark."

"You mean on track."

"Whatever. Trust me."

"Trust you?" The man snorted, but there was no humor in it. "You're the only thing I've got right now."

Monica let out an impatient sigh. "Steve, go get

107

some dinner and enjoy civilization while you can. You'll be back in that stupid jungle of yours very soon."

"It's not a jungle, it's a rain forest. And I hope you're right." She heard a fumbling sound, as though he had switched ears. "I don't like this. It's not right."

"Look, I don't know how you survived being dumped in the water out in rough seas, or how you managed to just disappear for a year, but now is not the time to fall apart. If you show your face, the insurance money will be toast."

She was right, and she knew that he knew it. She wished she had another snort of coke and looked longingly toward the nightstand where long lines of it had been a few hours ago. Just a dusting remained. She wet her finger, ran it over the residue, then rubbed her gums savoring the familiar numbing sensation.

"I told you the only way to get to Liz is to rattle her. Making her believe you might be alive and someone is holding you for ransom will work. It's the only way." Monica slammed her fist against the wall in an effort to squash a roach. She missed and it scuttled under her bed. "She's too friggin' honest. If she knew you were alive, she'd give back the money."

"I know, I know." A long silence deadened the air. Then he added, "I just hate deceiving her, hurting her. She mourned for me."

"She's over it, pal. She got herself a new boyfriend and they sold most of your shit. Your boat will be next. They're spending your money like there's no today."

"You mean—never mind."

"You have to play dead here. Don't screw this up for me."

"Just make sure she doesn't get hurt, Monica. I mean physically. If that happens, I'll never forgive you. In fact, you'll be sorry."

"Hell, I'm sorry right now. Sorry you came back from the dead."

Monica had nearly fallen off the dock when she spotted him looking over his old boat. She had let out a surprised yelp and quickly hustled him off the pier. His original plan had been simple, and he laid it all out for her over a cold beer. The schmuck was going to just show up on Liz's doorstep with his stupid-ass story. It wasn't like he wanted to start up where they left off or anything; he was married now and living in some stupid foreign country. What he wanted was for Liz to give him back his boat and his condo, which she inherited when he died, so he could sell them and take the money to his new life. What a dumb shit.

"Whatever you're scheming, it's probably illegal," Steve said. "Not to mention unethical, immoral, dishonorable, corrupt, depraved, and just plain wrong."

There was no *probably* about it, but Monica hadn't exactly told Steve the whole plan.

"Well, look at you, la-de-da, using that fancy college degree of yours with all them words. You know damn well cheating the insurance company is illegal. Don't act the innocent with me."

The line remained silent for close to a minute. Monica decided to turn the screw a bit tighter.

"And you? You took the coward's way out letting me do the dirty work. Now you're trying to rub my nose in the mud? That's some shit."

"You're right," he said quietly. Another long silence followed. She could hear him breathing. "I'm not proud of it. The only reason I went along with this dumb plan, whatever it is, is because the insurance money is all that's left."

"We've been over and over this, Steve. Back off and let me work it," Monica said irritably, suddenly tired of babysitting this guy.

The dial tone came on and Monica knew he had hung up. She held the phone away from her face. "Well, good night to you, too." She fell back on her bed. "Dante, you better find Richard or we're all screwed."

Chapter 16

A $6 Coffee and a 99-cent Burger

Dante had not only found Richard and taken care of that problem, he had the computer in his possession and had no plans to take it back to Monica. After sleeping on the beach a while, taking a swim to wash up, then stealing a soda and sandwich from some tourist's basket, he made his way to a bookstore/coffee shop and settled himself by an electrical plug with his back to a wall. Buying a six-dollar coffee had bought him as much time as he wanted, but he soon realized he would need a lot more time to try to figure this whole thing out. It wasn't like he could ask anybody for help.

Sipping his now stone-cold coffee, he studied the screen in front of him on the table. He knew very little about computers. He had been pushing buttons and trying keys for hours with no luck. Although seated at the last table in the corner, way in the back of the store, one of the bookstore employees managed to brush past his table and send his coffee and napkin flying.

"Oh, I'm so sorry, sir," the girl said, bending down to clean up. When she met his scowl under the table, she hastily backed up and bumped her head. Dante hadn't shaved and, even at his best, he looked scary. Deciding it wasn't the greatest idea to frighten the help, he wiped the glare off his face and forced a change in his demeanor.

"That's okay. Here, let me get it," he said, softening his voice as best he could. He reached over and took the rubbish out of her hand. The girl seemed to relax a bit and even gave him a timid smile. Her name tag read "Logan."

"Logan, huh?" Making small talk put a drain on Dante's limited patience, but he forced himself to be nice. "That's an unusual name. Like the airport?"

"Yeah, like the airport. Only it was my grandmother's maiden name. That's how I got it." She gingerly rubbed the back of her head.

"You okay?" he said, not really caring if she was or not. "That's a hard table." To emphasize the fact, he rapped his knuckles on the edge.

"Yeah, I'm okay." She nodded toward his computer, "You've been working hard all afternoon. Getting the job done?"

His gaze traveled to the front of the store where the windows were. It was getting late, getting dark.

"I need to get back to work here." Dante said, dismissing her with a gesture to the laptop.

"Why don't you let me freshen that coffee for you?" she asked.

"No, I don't—" He hesitated, not wanting to tell her he didn't have enough money. Even though he worked, drugs put a constant drain on his finances.

"No charge. Merry Christmas," she smiled. She retreated to the front of the store to the café.

Dante's stomach growled, but he couldn't afford anything in this store. He packed up the computer and took his new hot coffee across the street to the 99-cent burger joint. While he ate dinner, a few raindrops hit the window. It would be a wet night. Finding somewhere to sleep tonight became his next chore. The boat he worked on was in dry dock until after the holidays, so he couldn't stay there. He sure as shit couldn't go back to Monica's. Dirt had taken off hours ago, oblivious to Dante's real plan, which was to figure out how this scam worked and take it over himself.

It had become totally dark by the time he finally finished eating. He decided to wander over by the high-rise area and see if any of the beach houses on the side streets had left a garage door unlocked or open. A light rain threatened the laptop, and he shielded it under his shirt. A sudden yearning for a fat line of cocaine caught him off guard and made his mouth go dry. The desire touched him with familiar cold fingers, and he shivered. The first time he had gone to prison, a counselor had told him that doing drugs was like putting a gun in your mouth. But what if you liked the taste of metal? He closed his eyes a moment, thinking about the bag of powder he had so generously left with Monica. *Keep on track*, he warned himself. *Forget that shit.*

Across the street, he spotted a lady out walking her dog in front of a huge condo building. The pooch had on a shiny collar and a pink ribbon on one ear. The lady talked loudly on a cell phone. Gold sparkled from her wrist. Whistling softly, Dante crossed the street and got in step behind her, but when the lady let herself back into the secured entrance, Dante wasn't able to slip in with her. The rain became heavier. He flattened himself against the building under the front awning for protection, but had to move on when he saw a security guard coming his way.

He jogged around to the back of the building and was rewarded with a huge garage gate lifting to let in a car. Maneuvering under the gate easily as the car slid past, he kept his head down and made his way to the maintenance room which was only a few feet from the rear entrance door to the residences. From this darkened room, he quickly realized he had the perfect spot to watch people approach the locked door to the main lobby and use their key to gain entry. He studied the cars in the secured parking area. Newer models, well kept. These people had money. His plan changed from finding a corner to sleep in to getting enough money for a warm hotel. Carefully placing the computer on a back shelf, he found a good spot to wait. Lurking in the shadows, spy-like, felt exhilarating and got his heart pumping. He fought to remain perfectly still, watching for the right victim to come along, anxious to have this over with so he could boogey on down the road.

A woman would be good. An old man would be better. Time passed. He waited. A number of cars had driven through the security gate and found their parking spots. Still he waited. Lots of people had walked by him laughing and carrying packages, unaware he stood so close. Something had been wrong with each one of them. Too young. Not rich looking. Too many of them. He gripped the door handle so tightly, his fingers hurt. Trying to relax, he passed the time by thinking of all the stuff he would buy with that money from the scam. A new car. Nice clothes. Hell, maybe he'd even buy a unit in this very building. That thought amused him, and he stifled a chuckle.

The light sound of footsteps brought his attention back to the business at hand. And there she was. And she was perfect. Well dressed, she carried a large purse, and had lots of packages to occupy her mind while she approached the main door. Just as she placed her key into the lock, Dante grabbed her and pulled her into the maintenance room. Her hairspray went up his nose and caught in his throat. She dropped her packages and struggled, but she was no match for him. He had his hand clamped so tightly over her mouth he felt it when her dentures moved.

"Don't struggle. I won't hurt you," he whispered

in her ear. "I just want your purse."

She stopped struggling, but her body still shuddered.

"I'm going to let you go. When I do, you don't scream, okay?"

He waited for her to nod her head. It came in short, jabbing motions.

"I want you to drop your purse and walk away. You can call the police when you get upstairs. We still okay?"

Another burst of head movement. Her entire body trembled. It empowered him.

He slowly released his grip, gauging her movements, ready to re-grab her if need be. When she was totally free, she stepped away from him, but kept her back to him.

"I'm not looking at you," she said, her fear making her words breathy. She took a shaky step forward and gripped the wall for support. As far as Dante could tell, she never even saw the hammer.

Chapter 17

Walking Stiff

Renee bent down and picked the bracelet up off the garage floor. She held it to the light and admired the delicately woven links.

"I think this is Italian," she commented, showing it to Hanif, who turned it over and over in his hands, scrutinizing it closely. She fastened it onto her wrist. "Someone is going to be upset when they realize this is missing. I'll give it to security after we lug the Christmas tree upstairs." She headed toward the back of the parking area. "The storage room is down here."

"Hey, what's this?" Hanif asked. He had found a hammer and hefted it between his two hands.

"What's that doing here? The maintenance man must have dropped it." Renee pointed to a small doorway on the opposite end of the garage. "Run down there and put it on the shelf in the maintenance room. I'll go unlock the cage and start dragging out the Christmas stuff. Liz will be here in a little while."

A few minutes later, Hanif ran into where she stood tugging at cardboard cartons. His breath came in short, nervous gasps, and his eyes were big and round. "You have to come with me and see this," he said, grabbing her arm and dragging her down the aisle of meshed cages. "There's a lady hurt in that room."

****

When Detective Graciano arrived, Renee sighed with impatience. "What? Are you the only detective in this district?"

"So we meet again. An assault and battery right in your own building," Anthony said, staring directly at Hanif. "Imagine that."

Renee bristled. "He's been with me all day. Don't even start on him."

The detective seemed distracted by something. Renee looked down and saw that her hot pink bra strap was showing. Was that sweat on his forehead?

Detective Graciano blew out a little breath. "I happen to know that he was alone eating chocolate cake earlier today," he said, challenging her claim.

"That was hours ago," Renee snapped. "So he likes chocolate cake for lunch, what of it?" She reeled herself in and stopped before she said any more. She tried not to be too confrontational, but this detective always worked on her last nerve.

She studied him for a moment. He looked pretty sharp today, pretty put together for a change. Work with law enforcement long enough, and you learn that nothing with cops is what it appears to be. Still and all, her heart did a little pitter-patter, and she was chagrined to find that she couldn't control it.

"Let's go see what the victim has to say," Graciano said. He pointed his finger at Hanif. "You, you come with me, and we'll see if the victim can identify you." He turned toward Renee. "You have a problem with that?"

Renee shook her head. "Do what you have to do, Detective, but you're wasting time while the real perp is putting more distance between you and this building."

The detective drummed his thumb on his pad. His cologne wafted over Renee, and she blinked a few times, trying to clear her mind. *What kind of woman would be having evil, lustful notions when her neighbor, poor old Mrs. Jarvis, was lying in the other room bleeding and maybe broken? I'll tell you want kind of woman. The kind that hasn't had her fancy tickled in a long time.*

"I wouldn't even dare try to tell you how to report a trial, Ms. Rose, don't tell me how to do detective work."

Renee eyed him for a moment. "Fair enough," she conceded. "Let's get this over with. I have to put up a Christmas tree. Liz is spending a few nights, by the way, if you need her."

"Good. Thanks." The detective seemed thrown off by her acceptance of his authority and her little, tiny bit of cooperation. He strode over to where the paramedics were finishing up with Mrs. Jarvis. Renee could be mistaken, but was he limping a little? He seemed to be walking funny. Stiff like.

"Stay outside this line," he said, ducking under the yellow tape that had been placed around the maintenance room doorway. "Crime Scene will be here soon to take fingerprints and photos."

Detective Graciano approached Mrs. Jarvis's gurney and squatted down so he wouldn't tower over her. Renee watched as he spoke to her in a warm, calm manner. She clutched her house keys tightly in her hand. He gently removed them, then rubbed the older lady's fingers where they had made red marks.

That small act of kindness touched Renee. *He knows what he's doing around women victims,* she thought.

"We'll take a full statement later, after you've been checked out at the hospital," Anthony said. "But for now, do you feel up to giving me a quick version?"

"In all my seventy-six years," Martha Jarvis reported, her voice shaky, "I have never been hurt, never had an operation, never been really sick even."

Her gray hair hung loose, probably having been pulled out of her bun in the struggle.

"At first, I was terrified of being raped, but he only wanted my purse." A warm trickle of blood made its way past her ear. She pressed a gauze pad against it. "He came up on my right side when I was putting my key in the door, grabbed me, and pulled me into the maintenance room."

"Did you get a look at his face, his clothes?" Detective Graciano asked.

"No, he stayed behind me."

"Okay, go on."

"He said he wouldn't hurt me, just give him my purse. He said I could go upstairs and call the police if I wanted."

"Did he have an accent?"

"Maybe a little."

"Could you tell his race?"

"Maybe Hispanic, but I'm not sure."

"Anything unusual about his speech?"

"No."

"What color was your purse?"

"Red leather with a silver clasp. I just spent all my money on last-minute Christmas gifts." She gestured to the pile of packages she had dropped. Several of the boxes had been wrapped in shiny green paper. Now the paper was torn and scuffed, and the ribbons smashed. "Only had about ten dollars left. I had a few credit cards in there. Some personal stuff, license, grocery store card, things like that. I was going to give it to him, gladly, but I think maybe I was too slow or something. Next thing I know, there's a sharp pain on the side of my head. It knocked me right down and my purse went with me. The strap was all tangled between me and the floor." Tears made their way down her cheeks making her nose run. She fumbled for a tissue.

"Do you want to take a little break, Mrs. Jarvis?"

"No, no. I'm okay. It's just that he was so mean, you know? I landed on some of my shopping bags, and I couldn't get the purse out from under me. He kicked me hard a few times, yanked the bag, and ran out. I couldn't get up. I was in shock. I thought maybe there was internal damage or something might be broken." She closed her eyes a moment, seeming to compose herself. "I lay there for a while, then the nice man with the dark hair came in and found me."

Detective Graciano made pages of notes as Mrs. Jarvis told her story. As he flipped through them, the paramedics prepared to move her to the ambulance. When they wheeled her past, he pointed to Hanif. "So, one more time, ma'am—and I want you to be sure—this man is not the man who assaulted you?"

"No, my word, no. He saved me." Mrs. Jarvis's eyes were warm with gratitude. "Bless him." She peered past the group and focused on Renee's arm. She pointed a quivering finger at Renee. "That's my bracelet though."

Everyone looked down at Renee's wrist, where the emerald and gold bracelet sparkled in the multiple overhead lights.

"This is yours? I found it on the garage floor." She undid the clasp and handed it over to the detective. "I found it," she repeated a little louder. "On the floor. I clipped it on so as to not lose it while we wrestled with the Christmas boxes."

The detective took the jewelry and examined it. Then he looked toward Hanif. "Did you handle it as well?" At Hanif's nod, he added, "No use fingerprinting it. At least four people have been touching it." Handing it over to Mrs. Jarvis, Anthony quickly looked over his notes. "Any last thing you want to tell us, ma'am?"

Mrs. Jarvis sat up on the stretcher. The blood pressure cuff hung loosely down her side. A large black and blue mark began to form on her arm. The coloring on her face remained pale, but she managed a little shaky smile that smoothed the wrinkles in her cheeks. "He was taller than me. He was kind of light-skinned." Her eyes drifted upward and to the left while she thought. "Oh, yes, I remember." She tapped her chin. "He had a huge mole on his face. I tried not to look at him, and I told him that, but when I was on the floor, I could see his face good when he bent down." She rubbed the side of her head and winced. "I'm not sure, because it happened so fast, but I think he hit me with a hammer. I only saw it real quick out of the corner of my eye, but that's what I think he did."

Renee visibly paled and must have let out a little gasp, because it drew Detective Graciano's interest.

"What do you know about this, Ms. Rose?" Anthony's voice became all business.

"Don't you first have to trick me into confessing?" Renee said, resorting to humor to try to ease the tension. Hanif's fingerprints were on that hammer by happenstance. She didn't want to get embroiled in this mess, but it seemed she already was. She cursed under her breath and jumped in headfirst. "Hanif found a hammer on the garage floor. I told him to go put it on the maintenance room shelf. That's when he found Mrs. Jarvis. I forgot all about the hammer, until she just mentioned it." She shuddered, genuinely appalled. *To think the guy hit her in the head with it.*

While Detective Graciano wrote in that annoying notebook of his, Renee's mind raced. Mrs. Jarvis already said Hanif wasn't the perpetrator. How far would the detective push this thing? He didn't like Hanif. He could make them both jump through lots of hoops trying to build his case. Then a thought came, and relief flooded through her. "Security will have a video of us coming into the garage and of me finding the bracelet and of him picking up the hammer." Renee felt suddenly thankful for the safety features currently in her building, and vowed to not veto the monthly request for more security funding at the next association meeting.

Mrs. Jarvis appeared visibly spent from her ordeal. She lay back on the stretcher under the guidance of the EMTs. Detective Graciano had just signaled her release for the trip to the hospital, when his radio chirped. He took a few steps away from the group, but the transmission came across loud and clear.

"Graciano."

"You almost done over there? We got a body at 255 Ocean, room 14. Can you take it?"

255 Ocean Drive was the tourist motel and bar across the street from Renee's building. Anthony had been gazing down at his radio, but now glanced her way. Renee's heart did a little flip flop. More trouble? Making sure of where everyone was situated at any given time was getting old.

"I can take it. I'm right across the street. Out."

Detective Graciano strode toward Renee. "It's turning out to be quite a day. Someone," he looked directly at Hanif and paused, "is on a little crime spree." He tore his eyes from Hanif and addressed Renee. "I'll need to come back later and take statements from both of you. I'm assuming you'll all be home tonight?"

"Yes, we'll be here, but we want to trim the tree, eat, drink a little. Maybe more than just a little. You remember the concept of socializing, don't you? Can't the statements be done tomorrow?"

Anthony considered the request. "Normally, I get them while the witness is fresh, but considering you two didn't see anything." He cut his eyes toward Hanif. "Supposedly, didn't see anything, we can wait until tomorrow. That will give me time to study the security tapes."

"Good." Renee hesitated a moment, then figured she might as well nudge her barrel over the waterfall. "Stop back after you're done over there, anyway. I'll make you something to eat." With that, Renee's icy heart slipped from the hook where she had hung it so carefully all these years.

If her change of attitude surprised the detective, he kept it hidden. He studied her face, peering into her eyes so long, Renee almost took it back.

"If this is a murder scene, I don't know how long I'll be."

"Come by any time until midnight." *That was almost six hours. How much time did he need to see a dead body?* Renee mentally shuddered. *Imagine having to go look at a corpse?* She felt a little sorry for him. He was attractive, sensitive, and even appealing when he wasn't growling at her or stomping around. She gave him a small smile. "I make a killer iced tea." She winced. *Why did I say killer when there's been a murder across the street?* She felt relieved when there was no reaction from him.

"I may need it spiked," he said under his breath.

"You got it."

A frown creased his brow. "Did I say that out loud?"

She nodded her head and added, "But if you're going to drink my rum, you'd better start calling me Renee."

"Why are you being so nice to me?"

"Can't I be nice?"

"Well, you haven't so far."

"Normally you're acting like a despicable person," she shot at him, but her voice held a hint of mischief.

"I think you're beginning to like me."

"Maybe a little." She rolled her eyes.

He fixed her with a smile so achingly genuine, Renee did something that she had stayed away from since her divorce, something she had put a lot of thought into avoiding, something she had carefully closed her heart to. She fell in like.

Chapter 18

Pizza and a Plan

Monica opened the door to find Dante standing at the stoop with a grin and a silver laptop. "Let's order some pizza."

"All it takes is money, dude." Monica hit the door with her hip and let Dante enter. Dirt trotted in close behind. "All I got is a six-pack of cola and it's warm," she said. Monica had lost her job recently and had put her last bit of money on the rent for the motel. If this scam didn't work, she'd be homeless.

"You don't need money." Dante dropped the computer on the bed and dug out a cell phone from his jacket pocket. Ordering four pies to be delivered to the nearby Surfing Hall of Fame, he explained to the pizza parlor in a polite voice that they were for students who were working that night preparing an exhibit. "There, see how easy that was?"

"About time you showed up. Where you been all day?" she complained. "I thought I'd go crazy waiting to hear."

"We was a little busy, you know?"

"We found him right off," Dirt said, then quickly shut his mouth when Dante flashed him a warning glare.

Monica hugged the laptop and gave Dante an I-told-you-so look. "I knew he'd be close by. Didn't I tell ya'?"

"Yeah, you told me. You're a frickin' genius."

Monica flipped him the bird. "Where's the letters?"

"We didn't find any letters."

She tossed her hair over her shoulder and threw a haughty look his way. "Did you look?"

Dante turned his full attention to Monica. His glare was a warning that she knew well. "We was kind of in a hurry," he said slowly, barely concealed annoyance making his voice raspy. "I didn't see you in there takin' care of business, so we'll have to plan B it. That okay with you?"

His proximity sent little shivers up her arms. She wisely changed the subject. "Whatever. We still ain't got no money for pizza."

Dante flipped his phone closed with a loud snap and slipped it back in his pocket. "Amateur. Come with me and see how it's done." He turned to Dirt. "Go down and get some ice outta' the machine." He opened the door and peered out. Seeing no one around, he stepped out and pulled Monica with him.

They ambled down three blocks to the Hall of Fame and smoked cigarettes at the front door until the delivery man showed up. Dante thanked him and informed the man that the pizzas were free tonight. When the man started to protest, Dante pulled out a gun and asked if there were any more questions. There wasn't. Dante and Monica then made their way behind the Hall of Fame building and followed the water line back to the motel.

When Dirt opened the door Dante entered with a flourish. "Ta-da." The smell of cheese and sauce temporarily masked the permanent sour odor of the messy room. Monica, sitting cross-legged on her bed, stuffed a huge piece of pepperoni pizza into her mouth and chewed happily. A sliver of grease trickled down her chin. She didn't wipe it, which brought a scowl from Dante.

"You eat like a pig," he complained. He threw some napkins at her.

"I'm hungry," Monica whined. The napkins fluttered around her, but she didn't wipe her face.

"This plan better be better than the last one," Dante said.

"Yeah," Dirt piped up, his mouth full. "That was a mess with you givin' us the wrong information."

Monica sat up and crossed her arms over her chest. "I told you the right name of the boat, Lucky Irish. You two went out and grabbed the guy off the Luck-O-the-Irish."

Their ill-conceived plot to kidnap the Senator's son the day of the fishing derby had gone all wrong. He and Dirt had ended up pitching Steve over the side.

"It would have all worked if you hadn't been such a crackhead. Did you set your sister up? A little revenge on her boyfriend maybe?"

"Hey, I didn't board the wrong boat," Monica argued. "I didn't even know who Steve was at that time. Just his bad luck to own a boat with a similar name that you," she jabbed her finger at Dante, "snatched."

Later, when she found out the guy who disappeared had been her sister's fiancé, well, that didn't hurt. Just one of life's bizarre coincidences that worked her way for a change.

When half her pie was gone, Monica groaned and held her stomach. She pushed the pizza aside and pulled the laptop toward her.

"Wait, let me see," Dante said, plunking down beside her on the bed. "You got a code or something, right?"

"Yeah, I tole ya' that. The dumb guy give it to me at the airport when I put my hand in his lap."

He watched carefully as she typed in a few commands. When the screen lit up, she tapped it with an oily finger. "Here's the e-mails. I knew that jerk would try to screw me. He sent a third one."

"How do you know Liz even got those e-mails? Maybe she ain't seen 'em yet." Dante shook his head. "For cripesake, clean your hands off. You're making a mess."

Monica wiped her hands on the edge of the bedspread.

Dirt, who had been eating at the tiny motel dining table by the window, came over to peer down at the computer. "I can tell if your sister got her e-mails."

Dante's chin fell with apparent surprise. "You can? You?" For the most part, Dirt was all preparation and no H. That he had some useful information came as a surprise to Monica as well.

"My sister used to send messages to her boyfriend all the time and he would pretend not to get 'em, but she figured out how to check that." After a few awkward taps, Dirt confirmed that each message was not only sent, but received, and that Liz had opened all three messages.

"Let's see what our boy Richard has done," Dirt said, opening the last e-mail. Monica read it out loud then read it a second time. She let out a grunt of disgust. "I told you he was a moron." They studied the messages.

"Well, at least he kept the ball rolling," Dante said. "He didn't mess it up so bad it can't be saved. We'll do a final e-mail and fix this." He tossed a crust into the trash can. "First off, we need to decide when and where the drop will be. Any suggestions?"

Monica slugged down a huge amount of soda and let out a belch.

"Somebody ought to put you out of your misery," Dante said. Monica made a face at him.

"Should it be someplace far, so we can outrun the cops if we have to?" Dirt said.

Dante let out a snort. "No, it's got to be someplace close. Think about it, you idiot. We couldn't outrun a school bus in that junker of yours."

Dirt bristled. He pointed a bony finger at Dante. "Yeah? Well, I don't see you supplying no wheels on a daily basis. Next time you want something, you can take a taxi."

"We got to plan it so that by the time we get back here, the cops won't even know it's been done yet. There's not going to be any car chase." Dante appeared to ponder the problem for a few moments, then added, "It should have a lot of people around. No abandoned buildings or empty parking lots or stuff like that."

"How about the mall?" Monica offered.

"Too restricted. They got mall security, cameras. Only a few ways in and out. No good."

"Is it gonna be in the day or night?" Dirt asked.

Dante raised his hands, palms up, and leaned toward where Dirt was seated. "What do you think?" His voice became sharp and mocking. "Broad daylight in the blazing sun out in the open or under the cover of darkness?"

Monica could never tell what would set Dante on fire. She wished Dirt would just shut his mouth.

"Hey, just asking," Dirt said. "Don't take my head off."

Dante walked over and positioned himself right in front of the man. "No, no, I really mean it. I want to know. What do you think?" Dante stood with his shoulders pushed back, his hands hanging lose by his sides, his face grim. That was more frightening than him yelling.

Beads of sweat popped out on Dirt's forehead. He fingered his scar and looked to Monica for help. "He's messin' with me, right?"

Monica let out a huge exaggerated sigh. "Stop scaring Dirt," she said to the back of Dante's head.

"You know he's not the brightest flower bulb. Why do you have to be so mean?"

Dante rarely kept his temper in check with Dirt, but if Dirt was dumb enough to stay and take it, then frankly, Monica didn't care if he got the crap beat out of him on a daily basis. Just not in her room. "He helped with the e-mails, didn't he? Leave him alone," she added.

Immense relief showed on Dirt's face when Dante backed down and came over to study the messages again. Monica and Dante threw around a few more ideas. Dirt wisely stayed out of the conversation and went back to eating pizza.

"How about the fishing pier? You can see it from here and it's always crowded." Monica went over to the dirty drapes and pulled them aside. "See?"

"That's not a bad idea," Dante said. "Yeah, yeah. We could be fishermen. Those guys carry tackle boxes and stuff." He went to the window and studied the pier.

"The light's kinda' dim out there, and there's a line of stores in the middle that are closed at night. There's a lot of shadows, too, from the awnings." He grinned at Monica. "I like it, girl. We can sit right here and watch the cops scurry around like cockroaches."

"I don't want to be a fisherman," Monica complained. "I don't like the smell of fish and I don't like the bait."

"This isn't a pleasure date, Mon." Dante studied her for a moment. "But not a lot of women fish off that pier. Someone might notice a fisher lady. You have to be someone either no one will remember or a person they don't want to deal with." He walked around the small room a few times, then snapped his fingers and pointed at her. "You will be a bag lady."

"What? No way."

"Think about it. No one will bother you, and you

get to drag along one of those grocery carts the old ladies use. We can hide the money in there and you'll just wheel it off the pier. Who's going to stop a dirty bag lady and mess with her? It's perfect, is what it is." Dante seemed rather pleased with himself.

Monica shook her head. "Can't I be something else?" she whined.

"You half look like a bag lady most of the time anyway. It would be short work to get you in the part."

"Very funny."

Dante studied her a moment, his eyes turned dark. "You'll have the money, Monica. You will bring it back to this room and wait for us." It wasn't a question.

"Of course. What do you think?"

"I think you'd give up your mother for a buck."

"My mother ain't worth a buck," Monica countered. "This was my idea and I brought you guys in on it, remember?" She pouted a little and plastered a hurt look on her face.

"Drop the act, sweetie. You forget who you're talkin' to here."

"We'll split that fifty grand down the middle, just like I said. Then we'll go our separate ways. And no offense, Dante, but I kind of hope I never see you guys again. You know, fresh start and all."

"Works for me. How about you, Dirt? You lookin' to extend your friendship with the lady?"

Dirt grunted around a full mouth.

"He can sure eat a lot of pizza," Monica said, starting to feel a little queasy after her own six pieces.

Dante dismissed Dirt with a backhanded wave. "Keep eating, we'll let you know if we need you." He turned back to Monica. "Let's work on the last e-mail so there's no problem. And get a pen. We need to make a list."

After an hour, they took a break. Dante lit a cigarette and blew the smoke toward the ceiling. "You don't want to inquire as to your old boyfriend's health?"

"Hell no. Good riddance. He tried to screw me."

"He wasn't so hard to find. I just asked around a little. He got himself a room in a little motel other end of Ocean Drive."

Her face lit up and she punched her fist in the air. "I knew he'd be at the other end of the beach. I know that man like the back of my ass."

Dante stared at her a moment, started to say something then just shook his head. He cracked his neck in a most disturbing way, making Monica wince.

"So he got a room, huh? Must've pick-pocketed some tourist," she added.

She reread the newest e-mail they had devised, and they changed a few words. When Dante was satisfied, he had Monica enter the "send" details. Then, he personally pushed the Enter button.

"It's on its way," she said. Knowing Dante didn't know squat about computers, she snapped the lid shut. "I'm gonna close this down to save the battery." Dante didn't question it. Monica blew out a little breath and avoided his eyes. She held the to-do list under his nose to distract him.

"You gonna be able to handle this?"

Dante snatched the paper and studied it.

"We gotta get to an all-night WalMart and buy two identical wheelie bags, some fishing gear, and the other crap on here." He snapped the list with his finger. "Ain't no problem."

"Then it's your turn." Monica turned toward Dirt. "You gotta drive over to my sister's and leave one of them bags on her doorstep."

"Got it."

"But you gotta do it really late and really sneaky like, cuz she's having some party at her house tonight."

"Okay."

Dante pocketed the list and motioned to Dirt. "Let's get goin'. We got mayhem and mischief to commit," he said with a grin. "Grab a pizza, dude."

When the guys had gone, Monica locked her door and flopped into the chair in relief. She had deliberately typed in an inverted e-mail address so the message wouldn't really be sent to Liz. It was one letter off from the right address. She counted on Dante not checking it too closely, plus, she had diverted his attention with the list. She knew the message would bounce in a matter of minutes, so she had shut down the computer. Monica rebooted and pulled up the mail center. She changed the text to read one hundred stacks of twenty dollar bills, instead of fifty like Dante thought, and sent it to Liz's correct address. She rubbed her hands together in delight. A hundred grand. All for her.

Then she called Steve and told him it was on for December 23rd.

"Have you seen Liz?" Steve asked, his voice taking on a wistful tone.

"Of course, I seen her," Monica shot back. "Don't be getting all teary-eyed over Liz. She buried you and got herself a new man."

"I know, I know. But if the circumstances had been different..." he trailed off. A long silence followed. "Did they ever catch the guys who tried to kill me?"

Monica carefully kept her voice neutral. "I ain't never heard nothing. They think it was some drugged up bums out for your boat."

"But they didn't take the boat, you said."

"Then they must have been too messed up or scared. How should I know, anyway?" Monica wanted off this subject and fast. She steered Steve back to the story she had sold him. "Liz took it hard at first, but then she swung into gear. She buried you, wiped out your bank account, sold your condo, and now she's ready to snatch your boat. I just seen her today. She still has her pretty little house and her foo-foo dog. Don't be worrying about her. Worry about yourself and not getting caught and put in the slammer for twenty years."

They spoke for a long time, making their own list of things to do and planning their future moves. When they disconnected, it was just past midnight. Monica lay back in her dingy bed and waited for her heart to stop racing so she could get some sleep. The lumpy pillow had no case, but she hugged it anyway. With the dog stain on the ceiling watching over her, she wiped her nose on her arm and closed her eyes. Soon she'd be out of this dump. That is if Steve didn't find out she had been involved with his abortion of a kidnapping attempt, and if Dante didn't find out she was double crossing him and kill her first.

Chapter 19

A Warm Cookie

Liz sat on Renee's couch, Beans in her lap, admiring the finished Christmas tree. "It looks really good. I love the legal stuff." Twisted garlands of steno machine paper, little judge's gavels, and tiny silver handcuffs were mixed in with traditional red and green balls. Instead of an angel, perched precariously on the top was the Lady of Justice, complete with blindfold and scales.

Renee busied herself in the kitchen taking finger food out of the oven, a huge red mitt on her right hand. "I hope I didn't make a mistake."

The smell of warm dough filled the kitchen and she inhaled deeply. When Renee was a little girl, her mother's kitchen had always smelled like this on holidays.

"Cheese puffs are always good."

"Not the darn cheese puffs, the detective."

Liz put Beans on the floor and came over to the pass-through window. Leaning on the breakfast bar, she reached over and helped herself right from the pan. "Ooh, hot, hot." She jiggled the warm scone from hand to hand before popping it into her mouth. Beans was on a mission to find the cats. She systematically, but carefully, peeked behind each piece of furniture.

"You're thinking you had a weak moment, aren't

you?"

Renee pulled her hair straight out from her head in a rending motion and shut her eyes. "Liz, you'd tell me if I was doing something crazy, wouldn't you?"

Liz plunked down on one of the bar stools and wiped the condensation off the pitcher of Holiday Iced Tea. It had been spiked with three different kinds of liquor. "You talking about our cute detective or what you bought me for Christmas?"

Renee pointed the spatula at Liz. "You are going to love, love, love what I got you for Christmas."

A childish grin spread across Liz's face. She gave the presents under the tree a quick glance, momentarily distracted. "Which one is it?"

Renee tapped on the counter. "Not until Christmas morning, you big baby."

Liz put on an exaggerated pout. "Okay, fine. So we're talking about Dimples then." She refreshed her drink. "You got any more ice?"

Renee inched the ice bucket closer. "Snake."

"Was that always there?" Liz looked astonished. "I swear that wasn't there a minute ago."

"Keep drinking, girl," Renee smiled. "Tell me what you really think about Detective Graciano."

"I heard that he's a good guy, but a rebel. That he had a bad childhood and now he goes around doing good deeds, but sort of in a non-badge way."

"Non badge? What does that mean?"

"Like if he catches a drug dealer and the guy's got a hundred bucks on him, Graciano doesn't always turn it in like he's supposed to. Instead he puts it in the box at the homeless shelter. Stuff like that."

"Where'd you hear that?"

"Sonja told me. I mean, you can count on him to do the right thing, but his methods may not be entirely by the book. She said some con man took his family good, and that's why he became a cop, to catch bad guys. He especially hates crimes against women."

Renee considered this bit of information. She remembered how Anthony had tried to interfere when she tried to help Hanif in the courtroom and how he was convinced that Hanif was up to no good. She was beginning to understand his motivation a tad better. And she definitely identified with his little quirk. Didn't she just bail out a guy with the intention of helping him hide?

"He thinks he's everyone's father basically," Liz said.

"Maybe that's why he's so darn pushy all the time."

"Maybe. He's very dedicated to his job. Sonja says that's why he dresses badly. It just isn't a priority for him when some creep is hitting old ladies with hammers."

"Maybe I should ease up on him a little. You think?"

Liz wrinkled her nose. "Maybe just a little, but really you'd be doing society a favor. I wonder why his partner doesn't shape him up? She's so put together."

Renee nodded. "Did you see her bag? I think it was designer."

"I don't know what it was, but it was gorgeous." Liz took a sip of her drink and eyed Renee with an impish look on her face.

"What? What aren't you telling me?"

Liz put down her drink with a firm hand and waited a moment to answer, upping the interest factor. "Well," she said, leaning forward, looking theatrically from side to side as though someone might be eavesdropping. "Sonja also told me that your detective has a sister in prison."

Renee's eyes widened. "Get out of town."

"That's the scoop." Liz sat back in triumph. "She didn't say what sis is in for, but it has something to do with that crappy childhood thing." She drained her glass. "I'm going to have to take it easy on these, or I'll be in bed soon."

Renee produced another pitcher of amber liquid from the fridge. "Here, this one is just plain tea. What else did Sonja tell you?"

"Oh, interested now, are we?"

"If I break down and start seeing someone, the relationship better have a little substance to it, so the more I know about this guy, the better." Renee tilted her head back and stared at the ceiling. "It would be much easier to just back away. Why did I ever invite him here? Why?" She waved her hand in the air. "There's no such thing as happily ever after."

"You took the first step, and I couldn't be more delighted."

"Yeah, well, I'm glad you're happy. What about me? I'd like to know if I'm just a roll in the hay to him."

"I've seen the way he looks at you, and I think he really likes you."

"Oh? How does he look at me?"

"Like a man who's just been offered an unexpected piece of hot apple pie a la mode. And, of course, he'd like to get you naked and put a smile on your face. He's a man."

Sex. Man, it had been a long time since she had wobbled away woozy after sex. Renee needed a moment to steady her nerves. She peered past Liz to check on Hanif. He was still out on the patio watching the moon shine on the ocean.

"Back to your original question. Yes, I think you're doing the right thing warming up to this guy. There's worse out there, you know. And everyone isn't like your ex. This guy's got some good qualities."

Liz wasn't going to let this thing lie. Or die. Renee's divorce had been ugly, a ghastly entry affixed to her life's passport. The final hearing took place in the very courthouse she worked in, in front of everyone she knew. Time had healed her to the point of being able to function physically but she never got back 100% emotionally. When the dust had settled, Renee had closed the door to her heart, slammed it really, against her mother's best advice. Mom had said *Don't be afraid of a door closing. Another will open. And it could have a plate of warm cookies behind it.* Could Anthony Graciano be her warm cookie?

"It won't kill you. Just take it slow." Liz reached over and put a hand on Renee's arm. "You can't stay alone forever. It's not good. It's—it's unnatural, is what it is."

"What about you?" Renee asked.

Liz waved her off. "This is not about me. Don't try to change the subject."

As soon as it had come out of her mouth, Renee knew she was off base. Once her grief had subsided, Liz had eased back into the world of men without any problems. She just hadn't found anyone she wanted to get serious with yet. Of course, Renee had rationalized in her own defense, Liz's loss had been from a death and that kind of abandonment left less inner emotional scars and was easier to heal from than divorce.

"I just don't ever want to go through a divorce again," Renee said quietly. There was that word. It came out of her mouth, rose in the air, wavered a moment over her head, and drifted into oblivion. Maybe she would never have to utter it again.

Renee again tried to shift the subject off of her. "Wasn't Hanif funny trimming the tree?"

"He was like a little kid. I enjoyed watching him more than anything."

An odd sound made both women peer behind Renee. Beans had been successful. The two cats were diligently studying the dog from their perch on top of the washer/dryer. Noir, the female, menaced him with a low growl in her throat. Renee poured out some treats onto the top of the washer. "Here you go, guys. Merry Christmas." She flipped one to Beans, who caught it midair.

The intercom buzzed. A tinny voice announced that Renee had a visitor, an Anthony Graciano.

Liz smiled. "He's here. Let me put Beans in the bedroom then I'll take some cheese puffs out to Hanif. Give you a few minutes alone."

"Here goes," Renee said. She fluffed up her hair and wet her lips.

"You look great. Really. Go get him." Liz placed a hand on Renee's back and prompted her to the door. Renee smiled at the gesture. *Didn't I just do that to Liz a couple days ago?* Renee turned and gave Liz a quick hug. "We're a good team, you and I."

"You got that right. Now go. And try not to snap his head off."

After clearing the visitor with security, Renee slid the locks and stepped into the hallway. The smell of fresh pine was strong from the holiday wreath on her front door. When the detective got off the elevator, he looked tired. Renee had dated a dentist once, and he always smelled of Novocain. It had made Renee queasy and eventually caused their breakup. Renee worried for a moment that Anthony would smell of his job, of death. She braced herself for the possibility, but when he neared, his cologne floated out and hit like a little parachute of air, bursting pleasantly all around her.

"Merry Christmas, Detective." She didn't know if she should extend her hand or lean in to kiss his cheek. She didn't have to do either. He placed a hand on her upper arm and gave her a quick squeeze.

"And a Merry Christmas to you, Ms. Rose. Thanks for having me over." He smiled, but it only hit one dimple. He looked like he was going to bolt.

"My, aren't we formal. Can we relax for one night?" Renee frowned. "Or are you still on the job?" She hoped he hadn't changed his mind about asking more questions. If he brought out that irritating little book, she'd throw it over the balcony. "You can't possibly work 24/7."

"No, I get some down time." His smile deepened. "Renee," he added. At her invitation, he stepped into the warmth of her apartment.

"Take off your jacket and loosen your tie." Renee fought the silly grin that threatened to spread across her face. "Which is, by the way, kind of looking good tonight." She moved into the kitchen area and he followed. Muffled barks came from the back bedroom. As she took down a cocktail glass, Anthony waved to Liz, who was leaning against the open sliding glass door to the patio. He called out to her, "You're gonna' watch that dog, right?"

****

Renee looked spectacular tonight. She filled out her sweater neater than a CPA filled out a tax return. Maybe he'd get a peek of hot pink. The thought made a flush rise up his neck. He loosened his tie. The inside of her condo didn't surprise him. It matched her exactly, cool and pretty. Inviting too, so maybe not exactly like her. Although, she had broken down tonight. Anthony liked to think he had cracked her outer protective layer. It could be just the holidays. Or maybe his charm had started working. He brightened at the thought, then dimmed. Maybe Mars was aligned with Saturn and the fourth moon was in eclipse. As he accepted a drink of something icy from the pitcher on the counter, he glanced down at his tie, pleased he had taken time with it.

141

She suggested they move into the living room, a cozy candle-lit room, and sit in comfortable chairs. There were oddly shaped pieces of coral and piles of shells in glass bowls strategically placed between stacks and stacks of books. She must love to read, he thought. His brow furrowed slightly. *When was the last time I read anything other than a police report?* Violets in riotous bloom were on end tables. The window was a pleasure to look at with its lacey curtains and artsy paperweights on the sill. He looked closer at her Christmas tree with its small mound of shiny wrapped presents at the base. When he saw her decorations, a genuine grin formed. She is quite a character, he thought. She could definitely spark up my life. Quick snapshots of his house flickered in his mind. Empty. Cold. Messy. He had a moment of panic when he saw it through her eyes and realized he couldn't invite her there. How had it gotten like that? He'd have to change that. He'd have to change a lot of things. He sipped his drink, startled to realize he hadn't been paying attention to the conversation.

"Whoa, this is strong. Are you trying to get me drunk?" He smiled appreciatively at the woman before him. Oh, yeah, she'd be worth the work.

"Well, actually I've never seen a cop dance on a table, so I thought—" Renee shrugged her shoulders.

Anthony liked the sparkle in her eyes. He raised his glass. "There's always a first time."

"If you get drunk, you can always call a squad car for a ride home, right? So what the hell, live a little."

"That I can," he agreed. He hadn't given himself permission to live a little in a long time. How long had it been since he'd interacted in a social setting with normal people and not criminals? Maybe Grace was right. Not maybe, she *was* right.

Soft music played in the background, sort of

modern Christmas carols, easy to take, not corny. Liz came in from the porch and joined them. Renee passed around lots of tasty food—holiday treats and hot little pastry things he didn't know the name of. This was such a far cry from a few hours ago when he was dealing with gawkers standing along the railing of the hotel's beach bar hoping to catch a glimpse of someone else's misfortune. He grinned inwardly remembering how he had rushed away from the murder scene. Not that he hadn't acted professionally, but he had had the uniforms search the room and collect any evidence. Something he normally did. He would look over and catalog everything tomorrow, but tonight he wanted as much time as possible with Renee.

Anthony leaned back in the soft leather chair and tried to relax. He wanted very badly to be here, but at the same time, he had a list of work-related things he itched to start. He made himself focus on the here and now. The women had started telling funny stories about cases they had worked on. As he listened, he filed away bits of them. They would be perfect to relate to Grace on a long and boring stakeout.

"—he's not the kind of lawyer you'd mortgage the farm for—"

"—his getaway plan was to flag down a taxi—"

"—he only had one eye. So when they went to cut holes in the pillow case to use as a mask, he only made one cutout—"

"—he introduced her as his merry widow. I said, but you're not dead yet. He said, she lives in hope—"

"—he was a serial masturbator. Even his attorney didn't want to shake hands with him—"

"—someone had sacrificed a chicken on the steps of the courthouse. Everybody just stepped over it and went on their way, oblivious to the curse that had been placed on them all—"

143

The two women were obviously good friends, and he enjoyed listening to their easy way of interacting with each other. When one would start a story, the other would add a detail or embellish something, and they would both end up in gales of laughter. It surprised him to hear himself laugh. The easy acceptance of him into their fold pulled softly around his shoulders, touching him like a warm blanket on a cold night.

"Where's your partner tonight?" Liz asked, taking a break from storytelling.

"Grace has family. They do up Christmas big time, so she's off today getting ready."

"No family for you this holiday?" Renee asked this casually, but it seemed to him—and wasn't he a trained, professional, hard core detective?—that she appeared interested in the answer. For all she knew, he had kids, or maybe an ex-wife he was still tied to. He wasn't ready to spill the beans of his life yet.

"I'll visit my sister tomorrow." He didn't offer anything else. Renee watched him, absentmindedly stroking her neck with her thumb. It felt soothing and disturbingly erotic. His social graces were rusty, and he struggled to find something to say. He could hear himself breathing. Liz saved him.

"What is that great smell coming from outside?"

"The property is ringed with night blooming Jasmine. Isn't it wonderful?" Renee said. The scent wafted in through the open door and mingled with the vanilla candles. Maybe it was this crazy strong drink, but he began to feel happy, mellow even. He took another sip. "Is this drink legal?" *I should keep a pitcher of these in my fridge,* he thought.

Right at that moment, Hanif stepped into view out on the patio. Anthony hadn't realized he was out there and that fact hit him like a two-by-four. He thought this despite not actually knowing what a two-by-four was. Some professionally trained

144

detective. Had it been a serial killer, they'd all be dead. He stiffened as he watched Hanif maneuver about the porch, changing the direction of his chair. Anthony's gut twisted with his intense dislike for that guy. Dislike was too light of a word. Hate came closer. He knew he'd figure him out sooner or later, and get him away from Renee, but for now, he was determined not to let it spoil this night. In his mind, he and Renee were getting their first date out of the way. This could lead to bigger and better things if he kept it together and didn't piss her off. He knew he often came across as domineering and abrupt. It was important that she see another side of him. He mentally tapped himself on the forehead. *Concentrate on hot pink undies.*

"Let me refresh your drink," Renee said.

"You've got mail," rang out loudly from her office, stopping her in mid stride. She looked over at Anthony, a disappointed frown cancelling out her smile.

"Liz's cell phone is forwarding all her calls here, and we also left Liz's laptop computer on," Renee explained. "You know, in case." The dejected stoop of her shoulders and incline of her head told him she was not only disappointed, but ticked off. "She blocked all incoming messages except from Muffdiver3."

The night's pleasantries were abruptly over.

****

The e-mail had been ugly, ugly and harsh, and a slap in the face for everyone. Money had been demanded, not hinted at. And there would be consequences if it wasn't paid. It sobered Renee and cast a terrible pall over the group. Liz became almost non-consolable in her misery, doubt and distress. As Renee watched Anthony handle the situation with professional clarity and composure, she considered them very lucky that he happened to be there when their night fell apart. However bossy and irritating he might be, he was magnificent in a crisis where women were involved. He knew exactly what to say, how to act, when to gather a victim in his arms for comfort. When Renee realized she had run a sponge across the counter for the fifth time, she busied herself getting Hanif squared away for the night in the guest room. Then, with the help of a mild sedative, they got Liz settled in Renee's king-sized bed.

When Liz began snoring lightly, Renee retreated to the living room couch, mentally and physically drained. Anthony came in off the balcony, snapped his cell phone shut, and rested a hip against the arm where she lay sprawled.

"She conked out?" he asked.

"She's out." Renee covered her face with a throw pillow and rested her head back against the plump cushions. "That was rough." Through the pillow it came out, "at uz ruv."

Anthony peeled the pillow off of her face. "Yes, it was. How about you, how are you holding out?"

Although it felt nice to have a little TLC coming her way, she knew she didn't need it. She sat up straighter and pulled herself together. "I'm good."

"Yeah?" His voice came out low and seductive. She marveled at the effect it had on her libido. She could lie here all night and just listen to him talk. Then he placed a warm hand on hers, and she decided that was pretty nice, too.

"I want you to know I admire your bravery and your strength," he said. After a short pause he continued solemnly. "And I really, really liked your cheese puffs."

She playfully slapped his hand away. "You ate most of them."

"I know. What can I say?" They sat in comfortable silence for a few moments before he went on, "Listen, I'm going to figure out the best way to handle this. Let me work on it overnight."

"Okay." What else could she do really?

He stood, reached down, and pulled her off the couch. "Come on, walk me to the elevator, it's late."

It was a short walk down the hall. Too short, she decided. Renee became a tangle of emotions as she stood by the bank of elevators. She felt terrible for Liz, but she also felt safe with Anthony. Safe and something else. Something more primal.

"I'm so glad you were here," she said softly, leaning against the wall. Neither of them had summoned the elevator yet. She allowed herself the intoxicating pleasure of admiring his broad shoulders. His silky black hair curled over the collar of his pale green shirt, which stood open at the top. She could see the hollow of his neck and foolishly thought about kissing it.

Anthony took a step closer and placed his hand against the wall by her head. "You mean as a man or as a cop?"

Delicious shivers ran the length of her arms. She might need CPR if this lasted much longer. "Both."

She stood statue still, barely breathing, her heart thumping in her chest. She parted her lips, but no words emerged.

Anthony touched the pulse at her throat. "Your heart is racing." He smiled. "Why is that?"

"You're so damn close, I—" but she didn't get to finish. His mouth found hers, gentle and tentative and teasing. Renee closed her eyes and moaned softly, succumbing to the heat that melted her knees. She leaned into him, feeling the hard length of his body.

The sound of a door opening and voices down the hallway brought her back to her senses. She jumped and let out a small cry. Anthony straightened and pushed himself away from her.

"It's only a good night kiss from a party guest," he said, laughing at her nervousness. Flustered, she turned and punched the up bottom on the panel.

"I think I need the down button."

"Yes, you surely do," Renee said, fanning her cheeks with her hand.

The door whisked open. "I had a great night until.."

"Me too."

"I'll formulate a plan. I'll call you in the morning."

"Okay." At that moment, Renee felt certain he could handle anything. The doors slowly closed and he was gone.

She fought the foolish urge to go watch him walk to his car. Good lord, what had she started here?

Chapter 20

Making Coffee Nervous

For the average driver, the trip from Jacaranda Beach to the Abigail Kent Women's Correctional Facility, where Anthony's sister had been incarcerated, took two hours, but Anthony generally could make it in just over an hour utilizing his blue lights. This morning, the deep rumble of the engine and the vibration of the wheel beneath his hands soothed him as he made his way up the highway for his Christmas visit.

The monotony of the drive gave him a chance to reflect, to think about Renee and how he was going to go about winning her heart. Just like in his cases, he would analyze the situation and set a plan into motion. First he had to clean up his own act. When he got home last night, he had taken a serious look at his house. Just like his car and his wardrobe, it had been neglected for too long. In its current state, there was no way he could bring Renee there. And he very badly wanted to bring Renee home.

Left to him by his mother, this old Victorian was the place where he had grown up. On the day of her funeral, Anthony had come home to take care of the business of the dead and had never left. The house contained every memory worth remembering and many that could never be forgotten.

The front door still had the dent from the night

149

his dad smashed it against the handrail with his suitcase, got in the family car, and rolled out of their lives. The missing spot on the plank floor in the dining room came from the day the police came and took his sister away. In the ensuing scuffle, the handcuffs had gouged out a chunk of wood. The blood stain on the grooves in the kitchen counter was from the time his mother caught him pouring her gin down the sink. In the fight for the bottle, it had smashed and cut her arm to the bone.

Well after midnight found Anthony staring out into the darkened back yard through faded blue-checked curtains. He could remember when those curtains were new, when his mother had hung them, when they had been a family. Every so often, he considered selling the property, but his father's name still appeared on the deed, and Anthony wasn't ready emotionally to go through the legal hoops to have it removed. If dear old dad ever returned to make a claim, then the battle would begin.

A raccoon had made its way across the lawn. Lightning flickered as though someone were taking photographs of his trash-can party. Anthony sat on his back porch and mulled over the possibilities of his future. Would a woman like Renee, who lived on the beach, be happy here? He made a fist and tapped his forehead. Good grief, listen to him. He hadn't even asked her on a date and already he was worried about her moving in. But *would* she like it here? He wrinkled his nose and shook his head. Probably not. He thought about her condo, cool and pretty. Magazine pretty. But then again, she might like the idea of a garden in the back yard, rocking chairs, and pots of plants on the front porch. Located in an older section of the city, the street had mature trees, the nearby yards sported trim lawns and flowering hedges, and the same people had lived here for three decades. A solid, safe neighborhood, she might even think it was a nice change.

Change. That was something he would have to do. He found himself surprised that he wanted to change. With every fiber of his being he wanted to change. He could only hope he had enough fibers to do the job.

The latest e-mail to Liz Sutton had effectively ended their holiday fun, and Anthony had cursed its timing. It wasn't the first time a cop had comforted a victim, and it certainly wouldn't be the last. Before sleep claimed him, he had worked out a good plan and he was anxious to run it by Grace when she came in in the morning.

A movement on the road brought him back to the present. He maneuvered easily around a turtle making its way over to the grassy median. Maybe he could have a future with Renee, the sassy-mouthed, independent, feisty court reporter. At the thought of her, his throat felt tight and his heart ached with an emotion he was afraid to acknowledge. The ache in his groin was less confusing. Sure, she made him nervous, but hell, she could make coffee nervous.

He brought a finger to his lips remembering their short but memorable kiss. He had lain in the dark last night tasting her lipstick with his tongue until it was gone. Her lips on his hadn't lasted nearly long enough. That was something he definitely wanted more of. Instead of putting his shirt in the laundry basket, he had draped it over a chair because her perfume still lingered where she had brushed up against him. His hands, the same hands that routinely manhandled bad guys, had wanted to slowly and gently trail up under her blouse to the breasts that were crushed against him. Only by concentrating on the pattern in the carpet had he been able to stop himself. When sleep finally came, he was tortured by visions of pink panties and rivulets of moisture zigzagging down steam-room glass.

Checking his watch, Anthony pulled out his cell phone and speed-dialed Grace.

"This is Detective Slikowski."

"Slicky, I knew you'd be in early. Listen, I sent you the latest e-mail. You read it yet? Notice the difference?"

The first ones had been almost juvenile and silly. This one came across as cold, to the point, and contained no PS.

Place 100 stacks of $20 bills, unmarked with random serial numbers, in the black case that was left at your door. On December 23rd at 9:00 P.M. come to the Jacaranda fishing pier. Walk slowly, counting one-one thousand two-one thousand, down the right side of the pier to the rain shack at the end. Enter the shack and remain there until you are contacted. If you do not show up at 9:00 P.M. we will cut off one of Steve's fingers. If you do not walk properly Steve will lose a finger. If we see any cops Steve will lose a finger. Do not screw up. Come alone. We know who you are, we will recognize you. Steve will be waiting with his hand tied to a board. Think about that real good. Steve will be released when this is over and you have been a good girl.

"Yeah. It's from a different person all right. What do you make of that?" she said.

"I think the original writer is out of the picture. The John Doe at the motel maybe? Witnesses saw him working on a laptop at the bar that's now disappeared. It's a bit of a stretch."

"No, maybe not so much, Hang on a minute, let me find that photo." He could hear Grace shuffling papers, before she came back on the line. "The security camera at Ms. Rose's condo got a shot of Mrs. Jarvis's assailant. I can't see any facial features. It's just a guy walking in carrying a silver laptop under his arm."

"That adds up. Timeline is good, too." He started to get a good feeling. They were onto something here.

"Tony, the new writer changed the ransom amount to the exact amount Liz Sutton got from the insurance company. Now how did he know that? "

"So, somehow, this new guy knows the details of the insurance payment," Anthony said.

"And listen to this. Last night I pulled the old case file on Steve and brought it home. Seems his boat was named Luck-O-the-Irish. Guess where it was docked? The Blue Water Marina where Liz's sister, Monica, worked."

"Well, isn't that interesting."

"Not only that. The weekend of the fishing derby when Steve disappeared, the senator's son, a very rich man by the way, had a boat in the same contest. The name of his boat? Lucky Irish."

There was a pause on the line as Anthony let that sink in. Then he added, "Steve's boat is being held at the Blue Water, right? Until the insurance clears?"

"Yep."

"So Blue Water would be notified when to release the boat."

"Blue Water is a small marina. I got ahold of the owner and he said his only employee for the last two years had been Monica, until he fired her just recently."

"Hell, you're good. Are you up for promotion? You should be up for promotion."

"You're damned right," Grace said, "but that would make me your boss."

"Oh, that's not happening. So, a year later, Steve's boat is cleared for sale."

"Right, and the insurance check is issued, and Liz Sutton starts getting mysterious e-mails demanding money. Sis has got to be the link. Maybe the guy's her boyfriend. Or maybe she's got a little group of felon friends she plays with, and they're starting to fight."

"We've got to step up efforts to make contact with Monica," he said. "Did you send a uniform to her motel room?"

"I've already got her room on hourly checks. She may be ducking us. Office manager said he's seen her come and go a few times. She'll be brought in for questioning as soon as we find her."

"The condo surveillance video from Renee Rose's building, does it clear that Hanif guy?"

"It did. Their story checks out. You can clearly see Rose pick up the bracelet and then later Hanif finds the hammer."

Anthony tried to hide the disappointment in his voice. "Have the three of them view the dead guy's photo anyway, see if they know him. Did his prints come back?"

"Not yet. The only thing we know for sure is it's not Steve. DMV photos are completely different. I'll go over to Ms. Rose's when I'm done here. You'll be back after lunch?"

"Yeah."

"Okay. Anything else?"

"I left the crime scene early."

"Had a date, did you? Want to share?"

"It's not important." He wasn't about to tell Grace how he really felt. She would hound him for details. "I didn't get a chance to look through what was collected from the motel room. Take a peek at it, will you?"

"The evidence box is right here on my desk."

"Good. And here's another thing, requisition four thousand dollars in police money out of evidence. I've got an idea for a sting."

Chapter 21

All Men Are Scum

Renee woke thinking about Anthony's kiss. Pulling the soft blankets up around her neck, she rolled on her side, closed her eyes, and tried to recapture the moment. His arms had been strong and sturdy, his body hard as he pressed her against the wall. When she turned her face up to his, his mouth had taken hers gently yet firmly. There had been no hesitation, no fumbling. He had made his move, and she had given in willingly. It had just been a kiss, but it marked her, opened her up to wanting more. That feeling of being a desired woman warmed her blood. The ancient power a female has over a male swam in her senses and put a smile on her face. And could that be what she thought it was? Yep, there was a butterfly in her stomach.

She considered letting the day start without her, but felt too wonderful to stay in bed. *That's what love does for you*, she thought. *And it's not too shabby.* She dressed quietly and let herself out, heading across the street to the beach for her usual morning jog. Okay, her morning brisk walk. Okay, her walk. Truth be told, she hated exercise, hated that whole gym thing. In fact, filling out the application at the health club sort of winded her. None the less, she felt compelled to do something to keep her butt from spreading over her chair.

It turned out to be a perfect December morning—light breeze, sun on the horizon, air cool and salty. Renee passed a woman bent at the waist, picking through piles of shells, and an old man, with huge earphones perched on his head, methodically scanning the sand with a metal detector the size of a lawnmower. A piece of sea glass caught the sun and peeked out from under a lump of seaweed. She stooped down to collect it for one of her many jars. She turned the small treasure over in her palm. Its edges had been blunted by the tumbling ocean. She felt she had a lot in common with this piece of sea glass—both of them were worn down from years of friction. It sparkled a lovely dark green, the color of her detective's eyes.

Her detective. *Listen to me*, she thought. She rolled his name around her tongue and let it out in a whisper. Anthony Graciano. Tony. Detective Graciano, thank you very much. Wrinkling her nose, she looked out over the water, a deep blue today. Blue like a uniform.

Damn it. Did she dare get involved with a cop again? Quick, mean, little snapshots of her ex husband flashed up and caught her off guard. But, honestly, it hadn't been all bad. Like Liz, she had had it good for awhile, in the beginning, when he still did funny things and she was still his dream girl. With their own language, their own rhythm, it didn't matter if anyone else was alive. They had silly nicknames for each other and had made promises. Serious promises. Could she go through all that again knowing there might not be a happy-ever-after down the road? There were no promises with any man, any relationship, but with a cop? You could bet the odds, but everyone knew the house always wins in the end. A smart person would walk away from the table and pocket her chips.

Glancing up at her building, she could see Stormy and Noir sitting on her patio, peeking through the bars, patiently waiting for their breakfast.

Time to move on, woman. In more ways than one.

After her shower, she realized her phone message light was blinking. Giddy with the thought that Anthony might have called, she flopped on her bed and hit the play button. She felt a little tingle at the sound of his voice, but when the recording finished, a wave of disappointment hit her and left her frowning. He had left a message for Liz, but he hadn't even said as much as a hello to her. Could this be the beginning of many disappointments, or was she reading too much into a goodnight kiss? Maybe it was too early to get involved with a man again if such a little thing could dampen her spirits. Too soon? Well, hell, then when would it be the right time? And she had to admit for better or worse, she was sorely attracted to him.

"I'm just out of practice at this game," she said to Stormy, who had been twining himself around her legs. She bent to pet him. "I wish my life were as simple as yours, water in one dish, food in another, and a sunny spot to lie in." Renee decided to file away her feelings of discontent and readdress them later. Today she had to concentrate on Liz and the current drama.

Liz had had a bad night. Renee had heard her get up a half dozen times. Her door was still closed this morning, and she appeared to be sleeping in. Afraid to make coffee, aware the wonderful smell might wake her friend, Renee brought a cup of tea and a warm muffin out on her balcony and settled in a comfy lounge chair to enjoy the morning. The wind surfers were already out and colorful kites fluttered over the beach. The breeze blew her hair back and brought with it the tangy salt air. She turned her face to the sun for a moment, drinking in its warmth. Mornings like this made life worth living.

A squad car maneuvered its way down Ocean Drive past her building. Her mind immediately went back to last night and she let out a little sigh. She knew she was hooked. It would be hard not to think about him all the time. Renee's heart began to hum as she remembered how good Anthony looked in her condo, how fun he became when he relaxed. His smile came slow and easy and it devastated her. When he came near, he seemed to take all her air and she couldn't breathe.

Hanif appeared in the doorway with a corn muffin, butter dripping down his arm. "Liz still sleeping?"

"Yeah. You want to walk Beans? I'll sneak her out."

He flashed a big grin, nodded, and stuffed the rest of the corn muffin into his mouth. "Oomagh." Crumbs spilled out of his mouth.

Renee took that as an assent, cringing as he wiped his greasy hands on his pants—actually her gray jogging pants—and went to find the leash.

By the time Hanif returned with the dog, Liz was up and had begun drinking strong coffee. Detective Slikowski arrived to take their formal statements about both the attack on Mrs. Jarvis and their knowledge, if any, of the extortion being perpetrated on Liz. When the interviews were done Grace brought out a stack of what appeared to be old letters held together with a rubber band.

"I think you'll recognize these, Liz."

Liz took the letters and stared down at the little pile of blue envelopes. The paper had worn thin and the tops were ragged where they had been ripped open. It took her a moment to get her voice. "Where did you get these? These are from Steve," Liz whispered. "Oh, my God, where did you get these?"

"They came out of this man's motel room." Grace pulled out a crime scene photo and placed it in the middle of the table. Tapping the picture, she asked, "Does anyone know him?"

The three of them peered down at the glossy print of a skinny white male with dirty, blonde hair and pale skin. He wasn't looking too healthy.

"Is he dead?" Renee asked, already knowing the answer. She had seen hundreds of photos of bodies in her line of work. He sure looked dead to her.

Liz shook her head. "No, I don't know him. How did he get my letters?" She blinked rapidly as tears pooled on her lower lashes. Renee reached behind her for the box of Kleenex on the counter. Liz yanked out multiple tissues and bunched them in her fist. Perhaps sensing trouble, Beans came over, plunked down on Liz's foot, and leaned against her leg.

Grace directed her question at Hanif. "And you?"

Hanif shook his head slowly.

Renee turned the photo toward her and studied it, but the man didn't look familiar. Grace asked a few more questions of Hanif before apparently deciding she had gotten all the information she could.

Liz trembled lightly, thumbing through the pile of envelopes. "I don't understand."

"Someone got hold of these letters and used the intimate details in the e-mail PSs to make you think Steve was alive."

"What slime," Renee sputtered, outraged for her friend. Liz's head bowed and tears dotted the counter, despite the fact that she had clamped a hand over her eyes in a failed attempt to keep the anguish from flowing out.

"This male is deceased," Detective Slikowski confirmed. "Although Mrs. Jarvis didn't ID him, this subject is somehow involved in her attack. We found some of her belongings in his motel room along with your letters."

"Wait, wait. The same guy who attacked Mrs. Jarvis had Liz's letters?" Renee took a moment to let that sink in. "He was here in my building?" She was shocked at how close this creep had come to her and her friend without them having a clue. It unnerved her that evil passed by so close yet her instincts hadn't so much as whispered in her ear.

"He's dead? Who killed him?" Liz asked, sliding her chair back, putting distance between her and the picture.

"That's still under investigation."

"You mean this is the hammer guy?" Renee had trouble putting it together, and just that fact was strange to her, too, because she dealt with crooks every day. When it got personal, apparently everything changed

"So it's over? No ransom?" Liz crossed her arms.

"No, it's not over. He must have had a partner who double-crossed him." She pulled a copy of the latest e-mail from her bag. "Look at the wording of the last email, the grammar. It's different, cold. No misspellings. We think a second party has taken over."

"Why bring Steve into this at all?" Liz said angrily. "Why are they putting me through this?" She banged her fist down on the table, scattering used tissues and making the cats run. Beans scampered after them, happy to be part of the impromptu game.

"The most obvious reason is that if they can convince you that Steve's alive and he's in trouble, you'll hand over the money quickly and willingly," Grace said. "Think about it." She ticked off on her fingers. "The fact that they've never called on the phone when your number is in the phone book and easier to find than your e-mail address, the fact that they haven't answered any of the e-mails Anthony and I sent to them from Liz's account, never even opened them, the fact that they haven't let you speak to Steve, which kidnappers usually do to seal the deal, the fact that they're using details from these stolen letters to trick you. All that tells us there is no Steve.

"Maybe you know their voices. Maybe that's why they don't use the phone. They're sending e-mails on a stolen laptop using the PS information from genuine letters. It's the best they can do." Grace let that sink in a moment.

"We don't think Steve is in danger, because we don't believe Steve is alive. We're fairly certain Steve met with foul play on the day of the fishing tournament last year."

The room became quiet, the only sound the occasional sniff from Liz.

"With that said, Steve's disappearance was never officially closed by the police," Grace added. "Even though the insurance company completed their investigation." She pulled a few files out of her bag. "I have the police reports and some newspaper clippings here. His boat had been docked at the marina your sister worked at, is that right?"

"Um, Monica? Right. Yes. She worked there for a couple of years, on and off. That I know of anyway."

"We've been trying to get hold of your sister. We can't seem to catch her."

"She's a lowlife," Liz said, her face wrinkling in distaste. "Just look on any drug dealing corner, and you'll find her."

"When was the last time you saw her?" Grace flipped to a new page in her pad.

"Funny you should ask. She came over to my house just yesterday."

"Had she been invited?" Grace asked.

"No. Hell, no. She just popped in."

"Did she drive? Was anybody with her?"

"She said a friend dropped her off. I looked out the window when she left, but she just walked away down the sidewalk out of sight. I didn't see anybody else."

"What did she want?"

"I'm not really sure but when she left, my watch went with her." Liz's voice was tight. "Wait, she did have some story about having a job in Italy and that she needed to check the computer for …" Liz stopped abruptly. She narrowed her eyes. "She wanted to see my computer and go online."

"Could she have stolen those letters from you?"

"Sure, she could have. I hadn't seen her since Steve's funeral, but she was in the house that day." Liz's voice hardened. "That little bitch. Is she behind this, you think?"

"Well, it's a little early to say, but there seems to be some ties. She worked at the marina, so she knew Steve's boat had been cleared for sale, because the marina got the release letter from the insurance company."

Renee brought over the pot of coffee and topped off everyone's cup. Her own sister, Renee fumed silently, suddenly appreciating the fact that she was an only child.

Grace took a sip of her coffee then quickly took another. "This is really good."

"It's got a dash of cinnamon," Renee said, grateful for the break in tension. "Want a corn muffin?"

"Thanks, I'll pass." Grace put the files back in her bag, then sat back. "Detective Graciano will be over here in a few hours. He's got a ransom plan that he wants to talk to you about." She eyed Liz a moment. "We'd really like to catch these guys."

"Do you have any idea what the plan involves?"

Liz asked.

"I know he wants to put together a pile of money and go do the drop. He wants to run the scenario by you." She carefully set her cup down and added, "He may ask you if you're willing to cooperate by delivering the money."

Liz's eyes widened. "Me?"

"Isn't that kind of dangerous?" Renee said. "I mean, they killed one guy already."

"That's what the instructions say. They're very explicit in their demands. I think they want to keep you involved emotionally."

Liz's face became pale, her lip trembled. Her head shook slowly from side to side. "I don't know about this."

"We don't believe you'll be in any danger." When Liz didn't comment, Grace went on, "Liz, they don't want you, they want the money. If they wanted you dead, they know where you live." That brought a visible shiver from Liz. "They just want the money, but you don't have to do it. We can dress up an officer to look like you and see if we get away with it, but this may be our one chance to grab these guys."

Everyone sat staring into their coffee cups, each appeared deep in their own thoughts. Grace softened her voice and added, "You know, Detective Graciano, Anthony, would never want any harm to come to you." Grace leaned in, as though in a moment of sharing, and touched Liz's arm. "In fact, he told me he's crazy about you and hopes to ask you out after all this is over." Grace nodded and smiled, apparently thinking she had just delivered good news.

Renee stiffened and shot up in her chair. Liz choked on her coffee. Hanif just looked bewildered.

"What did you say?" Renee practically spit out.

Liz murmured "Holy smoke," as she wiped her mouth with a paper napkin.

A frown creased Grace's brow. "What's wrong? I thought you liked him. You invited him over last night for a little holiday cheer. I thought that little piece of info would be good news."

"How do you know that Anthony likes Liz, and he wants to ask her out?" Renee demanded through clenched teeth.

"Why, he told me so. Just a few days ago in the car." Grace rubbed her forehead and looked back and forth between the two women. Renee paced around the room. Liz looked stricken.

Grace gathered her things and quickly backed out of the dining area and down the hallway.

"We'll be back in a few hours," she said, letting herself out. The door closed with a soft click.

Renee cursed her bad luck with men, her hormones, her big heart, and Detective Anthony Graciano in particular.

Liz turned to her friend. "It must be a mistake, Ren, a big, fat, stupid mistake."

"No, it's no mistake. Think about it." Renee's eyes stung and she felt her nose growing warm. She stopped pacing and sat down hard at the table. The chair protested with a little squeak. "I only interacted with him at the front door the very first time we met, because he didn't want to come in with the dog there."

"But you two were flirting at the door," Liz insisted. "I saw it."

"It was just an awkward moment. I fell on him, for God's sake, rubbed myself all over him. What was he supposed to do?" Renee bit down on her lip and jiggled in her chair. "He and I fight practically every time we get close. Except for last night, I can't remember one moment where he hasn't been on me for something." She sucked at her front teeth and looked at the ceiling as one tear made its way out of the corner of her eye. She tried her best not to cry, but knew she would lose.

She went on, unable to stop the hurt from spilling out. "And he wasn't too keen on coming over last night until I told him you were going to be here." She raised the pitch of her voice and widened her eyes in a dumb blonde imitation, "Then he got all interested." She slumped back in defeat. "And last night he didn't sit near me, he sat near you."

"I was on the couch, you were in a chair."

"There's another chair right next to mine." She let out a slow breath. "I appreciate your attempt to make even the smallest thing work in my favor, but he was very quick to get up and give you a big hug when the e-mail came in," Renee said. "And this morning, he left you a message and didn't even acknowledge I was alive. And," she added, pounding the last nail in the coffin as far as she was concerned, "he told his partner. He told her he was crazy about you and when this was over, he couldn't wait to ask you out."

"But what about the kiss?" Liz asked weakly.

"What about it? It was a goodnight kiss, a thank you. You were in bed already or else he probably would have kissed you goodnight."

"No, no—" Liz started, but Renee wasn't having it.

"I read too much into it. I wanted it to be real."

Renee slapped her hand down on the table, making the liquid splash out of her cup. "Damn it. Damn it all to hell. I'm such a fool." She dabbed half-heartedly at the coffee spill with a crumpled napkin. "I told you, Liz. I told you I shouldn't get involved with any man and especially a loser cop. They're all scum. All of them." Renee shuffled over and flopped down on the couch face first. "What a frickin' disaster," she said into the cushion.

She rolled over and dragged herself to a seated position. Hanif started to open his mouth, but stopped when Renee pointed an index finger at him. "No, Hanif. Don't you dare side with that man, and don't give me any crap about needing love." She let out a long sigh and fluttered her hands at her face in an attempt to cool her cheeks. Everyone stayed silent.

"You can go out with him if you want, Liz," Renee said quietly. "It's not your fault. And anyway, it's obvious I'm not ready to get involved again. I'm such a jumbled mess."

Liz was indignant. "I will not. Never in a thousand years would I do that to you."

Beans jumped into Renee's lap, and she gently rubbed the little dog's ears. "You're lucky you're fixed, little girl."

Chapter 22

Sunny. Cloudy. Downright Chilly.

Two hours later, Anthony stood at Renee's door, a single pink rose in one hand and a piece of luggage at his side. When Renee opened the door, a wave of cold air washed over him. Little did he know it wasn't the air conditioning.

"Liz, your detective is here." Renee would not meet his eyes and her voice was brittle enough to cut. She abruptly turned on her heel and let the door slowly close on him. Slightly taken aback, Anthony remained at the threshold. Two heartbeats later, a savage jerk of the door produced Liz who asked him to come in. Renee stood in the kitchen, her arms folded across her heart, her face a tightly controlled exercise in discipline.

Anthony extended his arm with the flower toward Renee. "This is for you." A silly grin began to spread across his face despite his best efforts to remain professional. Although there on official business, he had hoped to get in a little personal moment before they started.

Renee stood stone still for a moment then said coldly, "For me? Whatever for?"

Anthony's grin fell off his face. She was clearly not in a good mood. "Ah," he stammered, "you invited me into your home yesterday." They both remained in their positions, fixed in silent battle.

She seemed to be fighting some emotion that he couldn't get a fix on. *Where was the funny, sexy lady from last night?* This was not how he pictured today would go. "I just wanted to say thank you," he added, trying to save the moment.

Renee reached over and jerked the flower out of his hand. Anthony yelped as the thorns ripped across his thumb. Renee slapped the rose on the counter so hard two petals fell off. Anthony sucked on his wounds and stared at Renee, not sure how to react, not sure what had gone wrong. Liz broke the moment by calling to him from the dining room.

Anthony nodded toward the rose. "Shouldn't that be in water?"

"It's fine," Renee snapped.

Whoa, Anthony thought, *a serious weather change here.* He tried to shake it off, knowing they had police work to do. He'd have to get to the bottom of this cold snap later.

"Is your partner coming?" Renee tossed over her shoulder. "She's one of the best detectives I've ever seen. I think we need to wait for her."

Anthony bristled. "She got called to attend the autopsy of the man we found in the motel. She won't be here, Ms. Rose." Anthony gritted his teeth and dropped into formal address. "But I assure you, I can handle this matter today."

Renee raised an eyebrow. "Whatever."

Looking extremely put out, Liz said, "Let's get this over with."

"Ah, sure." Anthony moved into the dining area and took a seat. "Where's the so-called student?"

"He's on the beach. Do you need him?" Liz asked.

"No, let him be," Anthony dismissed Hanif with a quick wave of his hand. "I don't need him, and he really doesn't need to hear this." Anthony didn't have the desire or the strength to get into it about

Hanif.

"Detective Slikowksi questioned him," Renee challenged. "She covered all the bases."

"Good for her." Anthony glared at Renee. "Now, if you'll let me do my part?" Renee jutted out her lower jaw but remained silent. *Let the sulking begin*, he thought. He had a lot more he wanted to say, but wisely stayed silent. He took a double-banded stack of money and placed it on the table. "This is what the stack of twenties will look like that we'll use to make up the hundred thousand dollars for the ransom." He gestured to the piece of luggage he had brought with him, a carry-on with wheels and an extendable handle. "This case was found by patrolmen at your house this morning as per the e-mail instructions. The bad guys want you to use this bag for the drop."

"So the bad guys were at Liz's house last night, just like they said they would be, and your department never saw them?" Renee said, apparently unable to stay quiet when she was so obviously agitated. She still stood in the kitchen, peering through the breakfast bar pass-through, keeping a wall between the two of them.

"We patrolled the area but, no, we didn't catch anyone leaving this bag," Anthony admitted, a little chagrined at that point.

"I see. So let me get this straight. You want Liz to go to the bank and get a hundred-thousand dollars worth of twenties, bundle them in packs of fifty, double-band them, and fill that case? Today? For tonight?" Her voice wore boots and they marched over his heart.

"You want to let me finish here?"

Renee fisted both hands but held her tongue.

Anthony tossed the pack of money to Liz. "Open it."

Liz ripped the two bands and fanned the bills

out. "Hey," she said, surprised, "this isn't real."

"Exactly. What we have here is a real bill on the top and bottom and filler fake bills. The filler bills are made out of the paper used for real currency, but they're blank. We got that paper when we assisted with a bust on a counterfeit operation out of Palm Beach last year."

No one said anything. Slightly encouraged, he continued. "I requested four thousand dollars in official police funds to use for the tops and bottoms. It's money we confiscated in past drug deals. Once we have possession of it, we're able to use it to make drug purchases and conduct other business of the police force, like this ransom. So, no, you don't have to go to the bank. We have this all set up. I had three crime scene techs do up the packs of money this morning."

He lifted the black case onto the table, unzipped it, and threw open the top. It was pretty impressive to see a bag full of money, and he expected the women to ooh and aah. They didn't.

"Okay, great. So Liz won't lose any money when this thing takes a dump," Renee said.

"Well, that's just a great attitude," Anthony admonished. "This thing is not going to take a dump."

The room fell silent. Anxious to keep the women interested in his plan Anthony waited only a heartbeat before launching into the details.

"They sent Liz the e-mails, they seem to have indicated a desire that she deliver the money." Anthony stopped. This was the tricky part. He took a little breath then rushed on. "If you wish to cooperate by delivering the ransom," he spoke directly to Liz, "we will have police officers all around you. Grace will be at the end of the pier nearest the rain shack. I'll be in the parking lot. Two other undercovers will be acting as fishermen on the pier. We will monitor you every step of the way."

"Isn't this a little dangerous, Detective?" Renee asked, the scorn in her voice unmistakable. "One guy has already been killed over this money. I don't think Liz should go anywhere near that pier tonight."

Anthony fixed her with a hard stare. She was messing up his plan. He tried to sound patient and wise. "The man at the motel was probably killed because he double-crossed his buddies. They don't want to harm Liz. They just want the money. They want Liz to be involved in this thing so she'll cough up the dough. If they wanted to do harm to Liz, they wouldn't have to wait until tonight. They could have taken their shot many times."

Both women cringed, and Anthony regretted his choice of words. Sighing mentally at how poorly this was going, he forged on, "They probably want Liz to deliver the money to keep her emotionally driven, so she'll pay."

"If you use a police woman and they realize it, do you think they won't take the money? Liz asked.

"It's hard to say what they'll do," Anthony answered. "In reality, I don't think they care who delivers the case, just as long as it gets there. I doubt they'd refuse the money when they're this close, but we don't want to spook them. They're expecting to see Liz. They'll be more relaxed thinking their plan is working. We want to nab these guys tonight, not have this thing play out again some other day."

Another long silence. Anthony let this one be hoping it might take the edge off, but he knew there was an awful lot of edge left.

"So what's your theory here?" Renee said. "Who are these guys?

"We're working several leads at the moment. I'm not at liberty to discuss this case further at this time," Anthony answered coolly, the hard set to his mouth making the words sound mechanical.

"Wow, that's impressive, Detective. Whatever are you doing in a small town like Jacaranda?"

"Reneeeee," Liz said, her voice rising, "you aren't helping."

"What twaddle," Renee snorted. "So in other words, it was Colonel Mustard in the library with the lead pipe."

Anthony slammed his hand on the table. "Enough already. What's wrong with you?"

Liz grabbed his chair and swiveled it toward her. "I'll do it," she said softly.

"Liz, are you sure?" Renee asked. "Let someone else do it. Let a professional do it."

"I'll do it," Liz said, a little louder, a tad stronger.

"You aren't afraid?"

"Sure I'm afraid, but I think he's right. They don't want to hurt me. They want the money. I want this over. And if my sister is involved, I want her caught and put in jail."

"Who told you your sister was involved?" Anthony asked.

"It's speculation from your partner, but I tend to agree. Monica's a bad person and lives a crappy life. I don't know that she's smart enough to be the leader in this, but I'm sure she's involved. I can feel it," Liz said.

"If all goes well," he held up his hand in a stopping motion toward Renee, "and I'm sure it will, then we'll find out tonight." Anthony appeared anxious to get out of there before Liz changed her mind. "Good, it's all set then." He neatened up the phony bills Liz had been playing with. "I'll come back at eight and brief you again before you drive to the pier. Just follow the instructions, hand over the money and let us do our jobs."

Renee let out a little snort.

"You have a problem, Ms. Rose?" Anthony asked.

"Yeah, I've got lots of problems, Detective." She said the word detective like there was a bad taste in her mouth.

"Anything that will jeopardize this operation?"

"No, sir," she said, giving him a smart salute.

Maybe she's bipolar and she's off her meds, he thought. He zipped up the case, hefted it off the table, and made his way toward the kitchen. "I'll bring the money when I come back tonight at eight, Liz." He gave Renee a hard stare from the doorway. "And you, you don't need to go. You'll stay here."

"The hell I will," Renee retorted. "My friend is not going down to that pier by herself."

"The e-mail said to come alone."

"It also said no cops," Renee countered.

"And she'll hardly be alone. We'll be all around her." Anthony fixed Renee with a hard stare. "You could jeopardize the whole thing."

"Don't be ridiculous. I'll sit in one of your unmarked cars with the tinted windows. No one will know I'm there."

Liz interjected, "I'm not going without Renee."

Renee had a triumphant look on her face. "I'm going."

"Fine," Anthony said, barely hanging onto his last thread of patience. "But you will remain in the car." At her look, he added, "I mean it, Ms. Rose. If you obstruct justice, I'll have you handcuffed and taken away from the scene."

"You bastard," Renee muttered. She raised her voice and her chin. "I would never do anything to place Liz in danger."

"You can call me whatever you want, but I will not let you interfere with this drop tonight. Are we clear?"

Anthony and Renee stood face-to-face scowling at each other. "Oh, you're perfectly clear, Detective. In fact, I saw through you the minute I met you."

"What the hell are you talking about?" Anthony abruptly showed her his back. "Never mind. I don't have time for this." He made his way down the hallway to the front door. "Just so we understand one another."

"Oh, I've got your number perfectly."

"Good," he countered, clearly not in the loop of this conversation, but not willing to admit it.

When he left, the door slammed behind him with a furious kick. Anthony pondered the situation as he rode the elevator to the lobby. It was like Renee Rose had an evil twin sister. He had so wanted to form a real relationship with her, and here she wasn't just high strung, she was a wacko. It was so disappointing. He shook his head in bewilderment at his bad luck.

He stepped out into the sunshine and crossed the parking area to his car. A pink rose sailed down past his shoulder and landed on the driveway in front of him. He looked up to the tenth floor where Renee's condo was, and although he couldn't see anyone, he heard a sliding glass door close with a shotgun bang.

Chapter 23

Bait and Switch

At a quarter to nine, at the base of the pier, everything was on hold while Liz threw up in the dune line.

"We almost set here?" Anthony said, walking toward the women.

"Does it look like we're almost set?" Renee shot back. She kicked sand over the vomit.

"I can't do it," Liz said weakly, wiping her mouth on a tissue. "I don't want to let everyone down, but I don't think I can do it. I keep seeing chopped off fingers." She tried to stand up, but her knees buckled, and she fell into a wobbly little heap in the sand.

"Damn." Anthony had positioned himself and another officer at a picnic table under the trees by the road, pretending to be tourists with drinks and boxes of fried chicken scattered around. Anthony turned and peered down the long fishing dock. He stared blankly at the other male officer who sat gnawing on a drumstick. "Maybe I can get a female uniform out here real quick."

"I'll do it," Renee said.

Anthony faced her. "Do you think you can? Do you remember what you're supposed to do?"

She looked at him with utter disdain. "I'm not an idiot. I was there at both briefings, Detective."

"You don't have to." This from Liz who was still on the ground holding her stomach. "Really. Maybe I can regroup." As soon as the words were out of her mouth, she turned and got sick again.

"I'll do it," Renee said again. "It's too emotional for her. She's not able to handle it. I'll do it." She turned toward where Liz had parked her car. "Let me just get the shirt."

Anthony placed his hand on her arm, a gesture Renee didn't like but didn't protest. "I've got your back. We'll be watching you every second, okay?"

"Yeah, well, let's hope this goes better than..." She let the words trail off. "Let's hope it goes well," she amended, heading toward the parking area.

On the dot of nine, Renee started walking, rolling the black case behind her. One one-thousand, two one-thousand. She slowly made her way down the right side of the pier. The bright yellow shirt, which Anthony requested she wear so they could better keep a visual of her, had already begun sticking to her back.

It was a warm, balmy night and the wharf was full of people; fishermen, couples holding hands in the moonlight, and tourists getting a kick out of walking out over the ocean. The lighting was dim, but adequate. The sides of the structure were lit and the water shimmered in yellow spots as the waves sloshed past.

Anthony sat trying to appear casual at the picnic area at the base of the wooden dock. He had a cell phone in one hand and a can of soda in the other, just a guy on vacation. Liz had been secreted in the car. Renee didn't know the undercover officers, didn't even know if they were male or female, but she was certain they were watching her.

The land end of the pier ran about fifty feet before it formed an oval around a row of recessed stores. They were all closed tonight, and dark, except for tiny nightlights under their awnings.

She had a small moment of panic when she realized she was coming up to a fisherman who had his gear spread out all over blocking her way. She would have to veer to her left and walk under the awnings to pass him. *Just breathe and keep moving*, she thought.

A man passed her from the opposite direction, and he nodded at her. It might have been a cop or just a person being civil.

Right in the middle of the fisherman's mess stood a bag lady, her rump in the air and her head in the trash as she dug around in the can. She produced a soda can and tossed it into her mini grocery cart. The cart was lined with a black trash bag and had all manner of stuff crammed in and around it. As Renee passed her, she noticed one shoe flopped from a broken strap. A feeling of déjà vu momentarily hit her, but she had no time to dwell on it.

She was now under the first canopy in a row of six. She concentrated on keeping her steps slow and steady. One one thousand, two one thousand. Suddenly a man appeared by her side, keeping pace with her. He took control of the handle of the rolling suitcase and they walked together. "You're doing swell, Liz. Keep walking as though I'm not here." A chill ran up Renee's arm, making the hairs stand on end. She tried to see his face, but he stayed just behind her. "When you get to the end go sit in the rain shack. When we're sure you're alone, someone will contact you in there."

They passed the spot where the fisherman had his gear in a heaped mess. Then they passed the bag lady who had now come under the awnings to sit on a bench and have a cigarette. When they reached the end of the line of stores, he took her hand and placed it back on the case handle. "Don't forget this," he half laughed, then faded back under the shadow of the awnings.

Renee emerged out from the store section and veered back into the middle of the pier, pulling the case and walking slowly, as though nothing unusual had happened. When she reached the end she saw Grace standing by the last light. She didn't dare make eye contact with her. Renee entered the shack and sat down, placing the case between her knees. She let out a breath she was unaware she had been holding. She had made it. All she could do now was wait.

****

Before Renee had stepped onto the pier, Anthony had studied the people on it, making mental notes. Dozens of men dropped lines into the water. Fishing rods stuck out here and there in bunches of twos and threes. Kids ran around gawking at the pelicans that hung around the cleaning stations, hoping for fish guts, a half dozen tourists milled about just watching the moon shine on the water, and a bag lady systematically went through each trash can in search of what appeared to be aluminum cans. Anthony remembered the bag lady arriving shortly after he had. She had made her way down the left side of the dock and by the time Renee had started her long march, the bag lady had rounded the end and had started back up.

Two fishermen had their gear laid out all over the place. They had tangled nets and open tackle boxes and several rods in the water. One guy had a huge tangle of fishing line. He messed with it awhile, then carried it over to a bench opposite while his friend watched the poles. The bench was under some awnings that ran along the six or so stores that were located in the center. The bag lady dragged her cart over to the same area, and Anthony could see the glow of a cigarette where she sat.

Anthony could see Grace at the end by the rain shack. She was on a cell phone, actually talking to him. Sometimes her voice would rise, and she'd say things like, "I told Timmy we'd go to Disney World this weekend. Daddy wants to do a little fishing tonight. I know, I know. I'll be home in a few hours." Other times she would whisper about Renee's progress. "She had to veer a little to avoid that mess those guys made with all their fishing crap. I can see her yellow blouse moving slowing along under the awnings. I can't see her face, but she's moving steadily."

Using binoculars, Anthony studied a couple nearing Grace's location. When they had passed, he heard Grace's voice in the tinny phone speaker. "Renee has just come out from under the awnings and continues to make her way to the shack."

Anthony watched Renee's progress as she moved slowly along the pier. Nobody seemed to notice her, never mind approach her. He saw the fisherman with the net give up and throw the mess into a canvas bag. He went over to speak to his buddy, and they started cleaning up their gear.

"Renee has entered the rain shack and is sitting on the bench at the back wall. I can see her through the window," Grace reported.

The bag lady finished her cigarette and pulled her cart back down the wharf toward Anthony. She stopped at the last trash can and gave it a cursory look through. She found one can and seemed to call it a night. She made her way off the wooden planking and rolled past Anthony and on up to the sidewalk. She slowly made her way toward the hotel area a few blocks down. Something dull fluttered in the back of Anthony's mind. He wished he could pin it down, like a moth on a specimen board, but it was illusive.

Grace was a patient woman, but after forty-five

minutes of no activity, she told Anthony she was going in the shack. He watched her step into the little building.

"I'm in here with Renee," Grace reported. "We're the only ones in here." A moment later, she said, "Hey, there's a price tag on that case. I personally cut that tag off this morning." Anthony could hear the sounds of the case being flipped it on its side and the buzz of a zipper.

"Shit, we've been had. It's full of sand."

Chapter 24

Bait and Switch, Take Two

Monica squinted to better see the departure board. She hopped from foot to foot in nervous anticipation, anxious to leave Florida and her old life behind. A perky airline representative approached, her starched red and blue scarf tied in an impressive knot around her neck. Her oversized, friendly-blue-sky name tag read "Ms. Chase."

"Can I assist you in finding your flight?"

Monica eyeballed the woman and immediately felt lacking. Not a new sensation. She had felt lacking almost every day of her life. Monica gathered herself, faced the woman, and gave the lady her best haughty look.

"Yes. I'm going to Hawaii tonight," Monica said, making sure her tone reflected the importance of one flying to such a wonderful place while this woman could only stand here and direct people. "I have a first-class reservation."

"Of course, ma'am." Monica watched Ms. Chase examine her shabby clothes, hastily donned and crooked wig, and the broken strap on her shoe, but being a trained airline representative, the woman managed to maintain her firmly affixed plastic smile.

Monica could tell the woman didn't believe her, and it pissed her off. For a brief second, she thought about giving the bitch a peek into her suitcase. Then common sense returned. "Let me see," the woman said, scanning the list of offered flights. "Yes, there you are. Ocean Air #567. It's on time at gate 35." Using that annoying flight attendant two-finger gesture, she indicated the departure security area.

"Thank you," Monica said, as though she received assistance from people every day and expected nothing less. "Now, if you will please direct me to the first-class restrooms."

Hawaii. A little squeak of pleasure escaped Monica's throat just thinking about it. Condos on the ocean and black sand beaches. Volcanoes and hula girls and fragrant leis. She would wear a flower in her hair and eat pineapple every day. A first-class ticket cost sixteen hundred dollars, but what the hell, she could afford it now that she was rich. The thought of all that money rolling along behind her produced a nervous giggle and put a spring in her step. A tiny twinge of guilt almost spoiled her moment, but she quickly squashed it.

Steve had looked so pathetic waiting at the hotel dock with his little motor boat. Waiting for her to bring him his share of the ransom. What a loser. He deserved what he got, which was nothing. This had been her chance, her time, and Monica gave herself a pat on the back for having the guts to pull it off.

At first she didn't want to dress like a bag lady, but playing the part had been pretty easy. No one on the pier wanted anything to do with her, and she had moved around freely. Her only moment of anxiety had come when she left the pier with the money hidden in her trash cart and walked past what she figured were probably plain-clothes police. The overwhelming urge to bolt had come close to taking over, but she had forced herself to walk slowly, shuffle along. Muttering and scratching, she had picked through rubbish cans on the wooden structure until she finally made her way up onto the sidewalk. Then she was able to speed up a bit, acutely aware that time was not on her side.

Her own motel room was four blocks away, and that's where she was supposed to go and meet up with Dante and Dirt, who had watched and waited until she had safely secured the bag in her cart before they started packing up their scattered fishing gear.

Halfway to her destination, Monica ducked into the Coconut Palms Resort, a fancy high-rise tourist complex, and quickly made her way around to the entrance that serviced the outdoor bar and hotel dock area. Once in the back, she spotted Steve on his boat and gave him a thumbs-up and then the ten-minute sign, holding up all her fingers.

In the ladies room, she quickly changed her clothes, donned a red wig that she lifted from the mall last week, and hefted the black bag full of money into a large green suitcase that she had paid the maid—who was an old buddy from her methadone clinic days—ten bucks to store in the adjacent utility closet. The hair color was necessary to match her new ID, a Georgia license she had found on a barroom floor, which pictured a middle-aged, plain woman with short red hair.

Heart pounding to the point where it grew painful, Monica had rolled her way by the hotel stores, past their steakhouse-style restaurant, through the marbled lobby and out the front door where she boarded the shuttle bus to the airport. It had been a scary few minutes sitting under the lights of the van, feeling exposed even in her carefully thought-out disguise. She kept the purse that she had picked out of a Goodwill bin clutched tightly to her body. Her right hand never left the handle of the green suitcase.

She bit her lip and kept her head down, not

daring to look out a window for fear she would see Dante peering back in at her with a murderous look on his face. The moment the shuttle had pulled out into traffic, and she realized she was going to make it, she almost peed her pants in relief.

Now all she had to do was fill her new purse with a few thousand dollars to buy her ticket and have some spending moola. Monica entered the baby changing room in the restroom area, locked the door, and hoisted the case onto the diaper table. The airport was quiet at this time of night, and she was alone in the bathroom. She unzipped the top of the green case, then did the same with the black case inside. She took a moment to appreciate her new found wealth. With a grin and a revived zest for life, she tore open the top stack of bills and started to count. Her jaw dropped open, and she stared in horrified disbelief at the plain green bills fanned out in her hands.

"No, no, no. This is not right," she wailed, ripping open a second pack, scattering the useless paper in her haste. "What the hell?" Raising her fists, she pounded the stacks of money, her money, her dreams, again and again until she was spent and had to step away to catch her breath. Bent over with hands on her knees, throat constricted, her words were barely audible. "That bitch. That bitch ruined everything." A fat tear ran down her cheek and plopped on the floor. Her nose started dripping. She swiped at it with an angry hand. Monica straightened, slumped back into the wall, slid to the floor in defeat, and sat on the pile of green paper.

"This can't be happening to me. Please," she begged any gods that might be listening. All her plans, all her daring. For what? Her luck ran crummy all her life, and apparently, it wasn't about to change now. If she had a gun, she might have used it.

A few moments later, someone came in to use the facilities, and Monica realized she had to get off the floor. She gathered the fake bills and stuffed them in a trash can. Then a new thought surfaced and the panic it created chilled her heart. Dante. She didn't need a gun. She had nowhere to go now, and Dante was going to kill her.

CHAPTER 25

Regrets, We Have a Few

The ride back from the pier couldn't have been more uncomfortable. Detectives Graciano and Slikowski were in the front, while Renee and Liz sat in the back of Anthony's unmarked car. A patrol officer followed in Liz's car.

"What a cluster—" Renee began, but fell silent when Anthony glared at her in the rear view mirror. With civilians in the car, Anthony drove carefully and within the speed limit.

"What happened?" Liz asked. "What the hell happened?" The back seat appeared to swallow her as she slumped back into it. Her face looked pale and tired in the fluorescent glow of each street light they passed as they made their way back to Renee's condo.

"They must have switched cases when they spoke to Renee midway," Grace offered. "We couldn't see under the awning section very well, but when she came out on the other side still rolling along, I didn't think anything of it." Grace fisted her hand and side-punched her door.

"At least they didn't get any real money," Anthony added.

"Right, so now they're really pissed off," Renee said. "You think that's a good thing?" Anthony started to speak, but Renee jumped in. She spoke slowly, her voice low and angry. "No, really. I'm not a trained police officer or anything, but that doesn't seem like a good thing to me."

He glanced back at Liz, but she was just peering out the window with dead eyes. Renee put a hand on Liz's arm. "Sorry, Liz," she said, "but what if we get home and there's a piece of Steve in her mailbox, huh Detective?"

"That's not going to happen," Anthony was anxious to quell the tension in the car. "Steve is not a real party in this fraud."

"Would you bet your fingers on it?" Renee quickly retorted.

"Yes, I would, Ms. Rose, because I'm that sure I know what I'm doing."

"Well, we did lose the money," Grace murmured.

"Et tu Grace?"

For a few moments, they rode along in stormy silence. Anthony could feel Renee's glare on the back of his head. He glanced in his rearview mirror. Her eyes pinned him with the sharp edge of her disappointment. Or maybe it was his own disappointment that poked at his soul. He turned in his seat and fixed Renee with a hard stare, desperately trying to think of something to say, something manly and wise. Something so enlightening and powerful, she would immediately shut the hell up for the rest of the ride in amazement.

The car moved forward at an alarming speed for a vehicle having no driver. Grace quickly reached over and took hold of the steering wheel. Anthony knew she wouldn't reprimand him in front of civilians, but her clenched jaw suggested she was biting back a caustic remark.

Anthony, frustrated because he had come up totally blank, totally useless, totally the jerk, finally turned around and removed Grace's white hand from the wheel. "I've got it, Grace," he snapped. "It was only a second."

Grace gave him the stink eye. "Sorry. It was the terror and fascination of certain death that got to me."

"Well, you should have closed your eyes then."

"What? And miss the crash?"

They pulled into Renee's property and eased up to the front steps. The women quickly exited the car, even Grace, he noted. Anthony stepped out and took a deep breath. If one was able to overlook the disaster at the pier, the night was inviting and pleasant. There was a promise in the warm, moist air. But, of course, it was not for him. Liz and Renee bolted for the front door.

"I want to get your statement while it's fresh in your mind," he called after their fleeing backs. He flinched when he saw Liz in the porch light and almost changed his mind. She was so delicate and vulnerable. But he didn't need to question her; it was Renee he needed to question. And, he sadly admitted to himself, still wanted contact with.

"Then let's get this over with," Renee said through tight lips as she and Liz made their way up the stairs and into the lobby.

Anthony could have taken her statement tomorrow, but she had been hostile the minute he walked in the door today, and he ached to find out why. He had asked around about her this afternoon. He had tried to appear nonchalant and acting in the line of duty and all that crap, but he probably hadn't fooled anyone. Nevertheless, no one that knew her said she was bipolar or crazy. In fact, except for the detail that she stayed away from dating cops, no one could give him anything unusual about her. He wasn't leaving until he had a damn good answer. After all, he didn't clean up his car, his house and himself all for nothing. Whatever he did, he was determined it could be fixed. He glanced over at Grace, who leaned against the car with her arms folded.

"What?" he asked, eyebrows raised.

"Don't you think we should call it a night? You and I were there, we know more than she does. You can get the little bits in the morning."

"Witnesses give the best statement closest to the crime. Criminal Justice 101."

"You just want to get near Liz."

Anthony didn't dare correct her.

"Making Renee do her statement tonight is kind of sneaky, isn't it?" Grace asked.

"You got a problem with sneaky?"

"No, not me, I love sneaky, but I'm beat. If you want to go up there and get your butt chewed off, you're doing it alone."

"Sure, abandon me when the going gets rough. I see how it is."

Anthony beeped the car locked and strode up to the front door.

"You're doing all the paperwork in the morning," Grace said. "I'm going home." She walked toward the squad car that had assisted them to this point.

"Oh, that's low," he said to her retreating back.

Grace shrugged. "No, that, my friend, is how you do sneaky."

Chapter 26

Neon Lights

After she had pulled herself together, Monica had removed the red wig and wiped off her makeup. She then removed the real twenty dollar bills from the top and bottom of each pile, except for the very top row, in case Dante peeked in the bag. When she was through, she had thirty-seven hundred dollars. Not a hundred grand, but more than she ever had in her hands at one time. It practically killed her to leave the real twenty dollar bills on the top row. That was another three-hundred she could pocket, but the thought of Dante's face if he opened the case and saw plain green stacks tampered her greed. She rented a locker and stashed the purse, money and wig, then she swallowed her fear and called Dante.

When he pulled up to the curb at the airport twenty minutes later, his face was dark with fury. "What in hell are you doing here?" he demanded, slamming the car door so hard it bounced back open.

Monica gave him what she thought was her best story, that the cops were everywhere, she was afraid, she dumped the bag lady outfit and boarded the hotel shuttle bus. But, of course, she ended up at the airport.

"I called you right away," Monica said, trying to control the quiver in her voice. Dante glared at her, grabbed the bag, and slammed it into the trunk. She noticed Dirt had wisely remained seated in the car. Before Dante closed the trunk, he unzipped the case and took a quick look.

"It had better all be here, Mon." Her heart almost stopped when his thumb ran over a stack of bills. "If there's even a dollar missing, you're gonna' be one sorry bitch." Monica thought she might throw up right there at the curb.

When he slammed the trunk closed, Monica made her feet move toward the back door. Dante stepped in front of her. His head shook slowly from side to side. Jerking his thumb toward the building he added, "You made your way out here. You can make your way back."

When he sped off, Monica moved from a dizzying relief to furious anger that he had dumped her, then quickly back to relief when she realized she wouldn't have to be there when he opened the bag and found out the money was crap. Someone was going to get hurt tonight, but it wasn't going to be her. What had she been thinking, anyway? She couldn't just go back home. She snorted when she thought about that stupid, dirty motel room. She patted the locker key in her purse. Now that she had a little money, she would find a better place. But she couldn't stay in Florida.

"To hell with you, dirt bag. Good riddance," she yelled to the retreating car, now just a dot on the road.

So here she was trying to figure out a way out of town. She scanned the arrival/departure board again, red wig back in place. The same airline representative approached with crisp efficiency. "May I help you find your flight?" If she remembered Monica from before, she hid it well. Monica's shoulders slumped in resignation. No sense acting haughty at this point. "Okay, so Hawaii is out. What else you got?"

Monica was impressed that Ms. Chase barely registered surprise. They both studied the board.

"Let's see, we have an 11:10 to Chicago. And there's an 11:27 to Milwaukee."

Monica wrinkled her nose in distaste. What boring cities. Cold, dull and lifeless. What would she do there? She was hardly listening to the woman. Her thoughts were on the tragedy that was her life but something the airline rep said brought her back into focus.

"Wait, back up, what was that?" she demanded.

"Flight 102 to Las Vegas, the red eye, leaves at midnight."

Monica lit up like a neon liquor sign and started grinning.

"Vegas," she said, letting out a little whistle. "Now, that's my type of town. I would be happy as an oyster there."

She headed to the ticket counter, once more, with a spring in her step. She could be a blackjack dealer. Yeah. She gave the ticket counter lady a song and dance about moving to Vegas, and how her belongings had already been sent, and that was why she didn't have any luggage. Her ticket cost two-hundred ninety-nine dollars. A bargain for a new life.

Chapter 27

Goose Bumps

"Aren't you scared she'll call the cops?" Dirt ventured, eyeing the open case of money on the bed in Monica's motel room.

"Nah, she ain't stupid. She'll show up here squawking for her share," Dante eyed Dirt and thought briefly about how best to cheat him out of his portion. "You know, I can't give you half of my share, don't you?"

Dirt's face turned into a frown. "What'd ya' mean?"

"I mean you didn't do nothin' in this operation except come fishing with me on the pier. I did all the legwork. I did all the planning."

"Hey, I dropped the suitcase. If we get caught, I get half the blame." Dirt jabbed a fist at Dante. "You and I are partners."

"Yeah, but I'm the senior partner on account of I've got the brains. You get five thou, my man. That's a lot of money."

Dirt appeared to consider that for a moment. He had to have known he wasn't going to win and actually might get the snot beat out of him if he argued. "Okay." He rubbed his hands together. "I'll take a smaller share."

Dante had expected a bigger fight. What an asshole, he thought, disgust clear on his face. Dante peered in the suitcase. The bundles were in stacks marked one thousand dollars. Dante reached in and grabbed a pile of stacks that had been tucked on the side. Most of the money was neatly piled in rows of five, five wide, and although he didn't know exactly how many deep, they were nice and deep. Dirt quickly stashed the loot in his backpack.

The noise of an engine turned their attention to the window. A cop car pulled up in front of their door. Dante closed the case and slid it under the bed. "Be cool, dude. Be cool. I'll do the talking."

The knock on the door, even though expected, made Dirt jump. Dante could see goose bumps on Dirt's arms and a line of sweat forming on his upper lip, which Dirt quickly rubbed off on his sleeve.

Dante opened the door.

Chapter 28

She's No Parade

"And that's when Detective Slikowski opened the case," Renee said, concluding her statement. She sat back and let out a puff of breath. Anthony entered a few more key strokes into the little black laptop, labeling and dating the file. He snuck a glance at her from time to time when he thought she wasn't looking. So far, there hadn't been any major fireworks, just a no-nonsense, cold, recitation of what she did and what she saw. No sense getting Liz's statement. She was in the unmarked car the whole time.

Hanif tapped on the sliding glass door. His voice was muffled through the thick pane. "Can I come in now? I have to pee."

Anthony waved him in then gave him a disgusted grunt. *Men don't pee, women pee. Why is he still here?* "Why is he still here?" He had addressed Liz, even though it was Renee's home. Liz shrugged in answer, then went into the kitchen to put on the tea kettle. Anthony was loathe to start a confrontation with Renee over Hanif. Although she had brought it down to a low simmer from what he experienced in the car, he figured one little wrong word would get him skewered, and he still hadn't gotten to the personal side of tonight yet. He was unsure actually how to transition to it.

The two cats sat perfectly still, side-by-side on the breakfast counter, alert in case anyone dropped a bit of food.

"You got a message on that machine," Hanif said, returning into the living room a few moments later.

"Thanks. I'll deal with it tomorrow," Renee said. "It's probably just the office with some back order."

Hanif gestured toward the balcony. "Back out there then?"

"No, we're done in here," Anthony said.

Hanif plunked on the couch and started flipping through fashion magazines. Anthony watched him a moment, then rolled his eyes in disdain.

Renee immediately jumped to Hanif's defense. "Magazines are forbidden where he's from. He's never seen them before, okay?"

Anthony didn't answer. He couldn't find any reason why Hanif couldn't be in her apartment, in her life. He fiddled with the backup file, then turned off the laptop. Liz began puttering around in the cabinets, muttering something about sugar.

It was now or never. In a few moments, Renee would be escorting him out the door. Anthony gritted his teeth and pushed forward. "Renee," he said, using the informal address, hoping to keep the conversation light, "Your get-together last night was one of the most enjoyable nights I've had in a long time." He hesitated. He had been staring at the table, but now raised his eyes. She sat studying him, but it didn't seem threatening. He continued before he lost his nerve. His voice floated across the table like a soft light. It was a voice a man would use with a woman he cared about. "And then today?" He opened his hands, palms up. "What happened between us since yesterday?"

****

Renee's first reaction was to rip him a new one,

but she quickly tamped that down. She studied him as he sat there waiting for her answer. His eyes told her he was being earnest. He had a death grip on the laptop. Renee relaxed a bit, realizing how sincere he seemed and how hard it was for him to initiate this intimate conversation. She realized he was having problems opening himself up and it tugged at her. She had problems opening up. Big time problems. A door slammed shut on emotions doesn't open again easily. She really liked him. He couldn't help it if he didn't return her feelings. Her heart felt like a soft, damaged place in her ribcage, like a bruise on a peach, that he kept poking. She did a mental sigh. At least she didn't have to deal with one of his gawd-awful ties tonight. It wasn't his fault if she read his signals wrong, but how should she word this so she didn't look the fool?

"There were some signals and some conversations—" she started.

"Yes?" Anthony leaned forward and wiped his hands on his pants.

"—that were maybe misinterpreted."

He looked confused. "For example?"

Renee scrambled for an answer that wasn't too embarrassing for her. "Let's start at the beginning. For example, you didn't want to come over for a Christmas drink at first."

"Well, I was working," he explained. "There was a body and—" He stopped. "That sounded a little defensive. I didn't mean it to be." He paused and when he continued, his voice became softer. "Usually, that's all I do is work. It was odd for me to stop and be social." When she didn't say anything he quickly added, "But I enjoyed myself, really."

"Well, sure. I told you Liz was going to be here."

"Yes, and she was." He shrugged. "And?"

"When you showed up, we got drinks and everything was going along fine. But when we all settled in the living room, you went right and sat on the couch next to Liz. It should have been a clue for me, but I didn't see it." Renee nodded her head at him like it should all be clear now. "I didn't want to see it, actually," she added quietly.

Hoo boy. Now she had gone and exposed herself. Was the hurt showing? She tried to make her face blank.

Anthony seemed confused. If he understood what she was talking about, he didn't show it. He started to say something, then stopped.

"You don't have a clue what I'm talking about, do you?"

"No," he admitted, "but I'm a good detective. I'll break it down and make sense of it. Let's get back to the couch thing. It seemed like a good spot. Did you want me to stand?"

"No, I didn't want you to stand." Renee let a touch of annoyance creep into her voice, then quickly squelched it when she saw him frown. She decided to move on.

"And you didn't leave a message for me this morning, you left one for Liz."

"Yes, I wanted to tell her I had a plan."

"So, I should have gotten that."

"Gotten what?"

She tried another tact. "It's very simple. I know when we first met, it was kind of awkward what with me falling on you and everything, but I..." she trailed off, not sure if she wanted to admit to him that she had been attracted to him physically. Normally, she was less interested in appearance than those things you couldn't see—kindness, integrity, and humor. But Detective Graciano had them all.

He reached over and put a warm hand on hers. She shivered at the intimacy. A little smile made his lips part. "Yes?" he urged.

Renee gathered inner strength. Her voice was so low, Anthony had to lean closer to hear. His scent invaded her senses like a drug. "And even though I haven't let myself get involved with anyone for a long time, even though I thought maybe I could never feel again, I felt something right then. With you."

Relief appeared to flood through him. He sat back smiling. "That's a good thing for you, isn't it?"

"Yeah, it's a good thing usually." She bit her lip and made an effort to keep the sadness out of her eyes. He seemed momentarily distracted by the lip biting and it made her smile. Men were so easy.

"So, so—" he looked around the room frantically, anywhere but her mouth, apparently trying to put a sentence together.

"And the kiss last night," she continued. "I realize it was just a goodnight kiss but it was—it wasn't..." she left it dangling unsure if she should tell him how it made her feel when he was really after Liz.

"Yes?"

"You probably shouldn't have done that."

"Was is too—"

Renee interrupted, "And then you brought me a rose today."

Anthony brightened. "Yes, that's right."

"That was a crummy thing to do," she shot at him.

"Yes, that's—what? But—but—," he stammered, floundering.

A tear formed in the corner of her eye, and he appeared undone by it. He fumbled for the tissue box and dropped it on the floor.

"It's okay," Renee said, giving him her best heartbreaking smile. "I was immediately attracted to you, and I let myself get emotionally involved with you before I knew." Spilling her guts was getting easier.

"Before you knew?"

"Sure. Well, I didn't know, but I was told."

"Told?"

"And believe you me, I was angry. And I took it out on you. But I'm okay now."

"You're okay?

"I'm fine."

"We're okay?"

"We're fine, too."

"Great." He sat back, a little frown on his face. "So let's end on that good note." He pinched the bridge of his nose and squeezed his eyes together. "I'll have to replay all this in my head when I'm alone later." He grabbed a tissue and wiped his brow. "Do you always talk in circles? It's very challenging."

"Detective—" She stopped when he shook his head at her. "Anthony," she corrected, "I'm tired. Are we done here?"

"Yes, yes. Let me just get my things together."

He began to put his paperwork back in the case and close up his laptop. "I should go back to the office to do damage control there. We lost a lot of money tonight and there's gonna be a ton of paperwork and lots of explaining to do."

Renee walked him to the door. He leaned against the door jamb and gave her a rakish grin.

"So, can I call you this weekend?"

Renee called him a pig before she slammed the door on his arm.

****

"What in the world?" he muttered as he jabbed the down button at the elevator. This woman would drive him crazy. Just when he thought he understood her, she jumped the track and left him wandering down the rails oblivious to the woo-woo. Well, he just wasn't having it. He was smitten with her. That's the best word he could think of. Smitten. And he would figure her out if it was the last breath he took.

He massaged his elbow that she had smashed with the door. She was no parade, but they were going to get down the street one way or the other, so he better throw his shoulders back and pick up the pace.

Chapter 29

Coal in Dante's Stocking

Two cops appeared at the motel door looking for Monica. Dante put on a huge grin and asked the officers to step in out of the warm night.

"Monica Sutton," the first officer repeated. He seemed real young, blonde. Still had pimples. "Is she here?"

"Uh, no officer, she's not." Dante closed the door and gave Dirt a look that told him to keep his yap shut.

"This is the correct address, isn't it?" Officer Pimples checked some writing on his notepad, then tried to pin Dante to the wall with a piercing look. Dante almost laughed. He had underwear older than this guy.

"Yeah, this is her place, but she's not here right now."

"Can you tell us when she might return, sir?" That came from his partner. He was a little older, a little wiser. More relaxed. He would shoot you after you answered the questions, whereas Pimples would pop a cap in your ass first.

Dante motioned them to a chair, stalling, but got a No, thank you, sir, to his offer. Frickin' cops were always so polite. Both officers stood firmly rooted to the spot just inside the threshold.

"I'm not sure where she's at," Dante said, his

mind whirring, looking for something to say to get these guys to go away. Then a lightning bolt of an idea hit him so hard, he could almost smell the ozone.

"We just dropped her off at the airport a few hours ago. She's going somewhere for a couple weeks. Didn't say where exactly." Dante kept his voice at a nice calm pitch, even though he felt cocky at the prospect of duping the police.

"Who are you guys?" Pimples asked. "Break out some ID, please."

Dirt and Dante turned over their licenses. No one said a word as they were scrutinized and checked via the officer's shoulder radio for wants and warrants. They came back clean.

"You want to tell us what you're doing here in her room?" Officer Calm said, handing the documents back.

"Yeah, see, we work the yacht down the end of the pier, the Ice Bear. She's getting her hull scraped and painted, won't be sea worthy until after the New Year, so our boss gave us motel and food money. But we said what the hell, let's pocket the cash and crash with Monica."

Dante watched the officers take in the room, measuring the veracity of his claim. When Dante saw the laptop on the shelf in the open closet, he momentarily froze, but the cops didn't seem to think twice about it. He was glad the fishing gear was in the trunk of the car. He made a mental note to dump that stuff.

Following their gaze around, Dante said, "I know it's a dump, but hey, it's free. You know what I mean?" Dante patted his front pants pocket. "We was just about to go get a steak dinner compliments of the boss at that all night diner down on Eastern Ave."

"What is your relationship to Ms. Sutton?"

"Friend. She works at the marina. We see her all the time when we pull in here. She said we could stay, she don't mind. We crashed here before." Dante spied the single bed. He was about to try to explain the bogus sleeping arrangements and thought twice. The less said the better. "We saved her cab fare to the airport."

"She didn't say where she was going or how long she'd be gone?"

"Nah, but we'll be out on the boat before she gets back in. I told her she'd have to take a taxi home."

"All right, gentlemen, thank you." The officers opened the door and stepped out. "If you hear from her before you leave, get a contact number from her and call us here," Pimples handed Dante a JPD business card with his number on it.

"Yeah, sure. Goodnight, officers."

When the door shut, Dirt fell on the bed in relief. "Man, you handled that great. I was about to piss my pants."

"That's why I get the big bucks," Dante said. "Let's really go get us a big fat steak." He dropped to the floor to retrieve the case. "I'm likin' that idea."

Dante felt good about evading the law, felt generous. "And to show you I'm not an asshole, I'll treat."

Dante flopped the case on the bed and unzipped the top. They both stared at their newfound wealth a moment, and Dante couldn't wipe the grin off his face.

"You think maybe we should go get us another room?" Dirt asked.

"Nah, our story is solid. The cops won't be back. And when Monica shows up, we'll tell her what to say."

Dante pulled out a wad of cash and broke the paper band. He started to count out loud. He didn't count for long. "What the hell?" he said quietly. Then he said it louder. He looked down into the bag and saw the stack of money underneath the one he had just grabbed. Blank paper. His face burned with anger. He dumped the money out onto the bed and rummaged frantically through the piles. All blank paper. Dante went over to the table and placed both hands palms down on it. He struggled to control the urge to smash the room to pieces.

"Well, hell fire," Dirt said, his mouth making an O.

Dante's shoulders were rigid, his breathing heavy. He stood still, trembling with rage. In an attempt to cool Dante down, or maybe just not wanting to get pounded when the shit hit the fan, Dirt offered to split his share 50/50.

Dante straightened and slowly turned around. "You couldn't see shit if you were in a sewer."

"What?" Dirt backed away from Dante's glare. "What do you mean, dude?"

"I mean, dude," he said the word dude twice as loud, "that your money is crap, too."

Dirt glanced over to the closet where his knapsack was stored. "No, no. You're wrong." He ran his hands through his greasy hair. "You gotta' be wrong." Dirt pulled his bag out from the back of the closet and dumped it out on the bed. Each stack held only two real twenties. "My money," he moaned. "All that for forty bucks?" He threw his knapsack across the room where it dangerously came close to Dante. He looked like he might cry.

"Check the bottom ones. Maybe they're real on the very bottom," Dirt said hopefully.

Dante sank down in a chair. "Ain't no real nothing in that pile of junk," he yelled. Then more calmly he added, "You are slower than my Tito Carlos reaching for the check, you know that?"

"Who did this?" Dirt asked. "Monica, you think?"

"That is the question of the century." Dante

stared at the stacks of fake money willing this to all be a big joke. His brow wrinkled. "There's too many of them."

"What?"

"Look at all of them stacks. There's too many."

"I don't understand. We got too much of nothing?"

Dante was no math wiz, but at a thousand dollars per stack, he should have had fifty stacks. This case had fifteen stacks per layer, with like six layers. What the hell had Monica done? Personally, Dante thought her too stupid to be able to pull a stunt like this, but then again, she ended up out at the airport and that wasn't in the plan. Maybe she planned to get out of Dodge with all the money. But if that was the case, why did she call? Dante hurled the case off the bed and gave it a viscous kick.

"When Monica gets here, she's gonna get her ass beat." He stormed over to the window and peered out. The parking lot was empty.

"You can't really believe Monica'll come back here," Dirt said. He sat on the bed and hung his head in his hands. "Who's the slow one now, huh?" he said, but very, very quietly.

Chapter 30

A Message from Beyond

Renee cleared the table then headed toward her room. "I'm going to take a shower," she called back over her shoulder. She noticed the blinking message light on her phone as she pulled out clean underwear. "Liz, would you see who called yesterday and take a message for me?"

Renee heard something over the sound of running water, but she couldn't make it out. She wasn't even sure the noise she heard was real. It sounded like someone wailing. She listened intently as the water jetted down her body. There it was again. She turned off the water. It was definitely crying. "Liz?" She threw on a towel and opened the door. "Liz, is that you?"

Liz sat huddled on the floor by Renee's bed. The handset to the phone lay on the floor. When Liz looked up, her face crumpled. "It's Steve," she sobbed. "On the phone. It's really Steve."

Renee dropped down on the floor and sat by her friend. She put the phone on speaker and played the message. Then she played it again.

"Man, that sure sounds like Steve."

"How could this be?" sobbed Liz. "How?"

Renee had no answer. She racked her brain trying to think of something to say to comfort her friend, or try to explain what they had just heard.

"That's the best he could do?" Renee said, suddenly and irrationally angry at Steve. "No I'm sorry, no type of explanation, no groveling?" She mentally added no I love you, I missed you, hope you're all right?

The man on the phone—okay, she had to admit it was either Steve or his clone—sounded pretty normal. A little nervous maybe—he cleared his throat twice—but not like a man who'd been gone for a year. Not a trace of guilt or remorse, or even relief to be home.

"Okay, let's analyze this," Renee said, trying to do damage control on the situation. "First of all, assuming it's really Steve—" at the look from Liz she hurried on, "and it sure sounds like it is, he's not hurt. Got all his fingers, right?"

"That's true."

Renee pulled the handset closer to her face. "Okay, so, the call came in—let's see—it came in two hours after the ransom drop."

"Yeah?"

"Yeah." She pushed the small lighted screen under Liz's eyes. "See?"

Liz just nodded. It encouraged Renee to see that she had stopped sobbing so she continued.

"Where do you suppose he's been all this time?" Liz said, her voice breathy. To say she was overwhelmingly stunned would be a small start.

"I can't even begin to imagine."

Steve wasn't the type of guy who would run away to the circus or join some religious cult. Renee glanced at the clock radio. The green digital printout told her they had twenty minutes to get to the park, and the urge to strangle Steve told her she believed he was very much alive. The thought that he might be involved in the insurance scam flitted through her mind, but she pushed it away. Liz was on overload now, no sense bringing it up.

"So he wants to meet at noon and tell you his story." She turned to her best friend and looked earnestly into her face. "Do you want to see him?"

"Hell, yes." Liz sniffed and wiped her eyes on the sleeve of her t-shirt. "That man has a lot of explaining to do."

She got up and pulled Liz off the floor. "Come on then, let's go talk to a dead man."

And this better be damn good.

Chapter 31

Dante's New Favorite Color

Dante leaned against his car and intently scrutinized the high rise condo that rose up sixteen floors in front of him. He downed the last of his cold coffee, crushed the cup, and tossed it on the roadway. A passing motorist gave him a dirty look, then quickly snapped her head forward, the decision to mind her own business probably prompted by the murderous look in Dante's eyes. It was close to noon and unbearably hot in the car.

Monica's little journal of information and pictures had proven to be valuable after all. Last night at two in the morning when there was still no Monica, Dante had to admit the bitch wasn't coming back. Either she had the money, or she found out the money was crap and ran. They had only gotten a lousy three-hundred dollars from the suitcase.

Dante decided he'd go after that cool fifty grand directly through Liz. To hell with that lying, cheating Monica and her stupid scheme. To hell with e-mails that hint of trouble. Dante would bring trouble right out in the open and kick some ass while he was at it.

He knew Liz's home address, they had left the bag on her porch, but when he rolled by at three this morning, her house was dark, no car. Monica's notes said she had a little dog. No little dog barking. When

Dante called Liz's home phone, he got a recording that said he had reached Renee and to leave a message. Who was Renee? Yep, there it was in Monica's book. Best friend, lived on Ocean Drive. The same building where he had robbed the old lady and across the street from the hotel where he had taken care of Richard. Life was full of interesting coincidences. From studying the photos, he now knew she was the one who made the money drop, not Liz. Stupid bitches didn't even follow the directions right.

Now here he stood nine hours later, unable to gain access into the guarded, gated condo. Renee lived on the tenth floor, so he couldn't burgle the place. Next step? Not sure. He had parked on the side street that faced the garage to weigh his options.

As far as he could figure he had three of them; muscle or trick his way past the guard, pretend to be a visitor and hope to be buzzed in, or hope the women decided to go out today. He hated all of them. Tricking the guard could result in the police. Pretending to be a visitor might not get him in, but would get him on the security camera. And lastly, the women might be happily tucked in up there with no plans to leave.

Dante took in his surroundings. It pissed him off. The grounds were immaculate. Flowers bloomed everywhere, lush green lawn areas, little bubbly water fountains with pretty goldfish darting around. This was the world he should be living in. Instead he was destined to stand outside on the hot cement looking in with big puppy eyes.

He cracked his neck and rubbed his eyes. Fatigue was setting in. It bothered the hell out of him, but he admitted he might have to go back to Monica's crappy motel room. After some sleep, he was confident he could come up with a sound plan B.

And if by some stroke of luck Monica happened to have come back home? Well, he'd have to spend some time teaching her to have respect.

Then his luck changed. A grin split his face and he suddenly jerked wide awake. Liz, and a chick who he now knew was Renee, came darting out of the gated garage in a little red sedan and passed right in front of him. After green, the color of money, red was now his new favorite color. Renee drove at a fast clip heading south down Ocean Drive. He banged his fist in victory on the hood of the car, startling Dirt who had been sleeping.

"Wake up, dude. The game is on." Dante's voice was almost giddy with relief.

"What happened?" Dirt let out a huge yawn and rubbed his puffy face. The dark circles under his eyes were so ugly they looked like bruises against his pale skin. "I gotta take a piss."

"Swallow it. It's time to get paid."

Dante started singing in Spanish, his mood enhanced by the jolt of adrenaline that zipped through his body. Jumping in the driver's side, he pulled out smoothly and punched the gas until he was able to find a place in line directly behind the two women.

"Is that her?" Dirt asked.

Dante almost took his eyes off the road to stare at the dumbest man in the world.

"No, Dirt, that's not her," Dante said, his voice tight with irritation. "I just wanted to follow these two women, maybe try to pick them up."

"All right, all right, you don't have to take my head off. I was just askin'." Dirt scratched his crotch. "Got any coffee left?"

This time, Dante did turn his head to glare at Dirt. "Pay attention here. This may be our only chance to grab onto Liz, get our money." Dante's good mood was dissipating fast. He pondered his bad luck at how a brilliant guy like himself ever ended up with a moron like Dirt.

"So you got a plan, right?" Dirt said.

"You looking for a pounding today?"

"Just want to know what the plan is, is all," Dirt whined. "Am I supposed to jump out the car and snatch her at some light or what?"

"I'll tell you what to do when the time comes. Don't do a thing, not one single damn thing, unless I tell you, you got it?"

"Yeah, I got it." Dirt sulked back against his seat and began picking scabs off the back of his knuckles.

Dante played around with the idea of pushing Dirt out of the car right in the middle of Ocean Drive. He dismissed the idea, as tantalizing as it was, seeing as how it would make a commotion. Not something he wanted right now. And there was also the possibility he might need the jerk to help handle the two women. He was definitely gonna have to take care of Dirt when this was all over. And not in a good way.

Chapter 32

Lots of Lover's Stuff

Anthony's radio crackled to life. "Dispatch to Graciano."

"This is Graciano"

"Be advised a male caller by the name of Hanif just called, says you need to get over to 1610 Ocean Drive right away."

Anthony's blood turned cold. That was Renee's building. The airwaves were silent a moment. Anthony keyed his mike with an impatient click.

"Is that it?"

"Said you need to hear a message. Said he was left behind, but he's going to try to run down and help. That's it. He hung up. We tried calling him back, but there's no answer. Records check shows the phone number belongs to a Renee Rose, apartment 10C at that address. The guy said he needed to get that message to you right away. Should I send a unit?"

"No, I'm close. I'm on my way. Radio Detective Slikowski to meet me there code 3."

"Roger that. Out."

Anthony abandoned the coffee he had been putting sugar in and took off toward the door. "I'll be back to pay for that," he threw over his shoulder as he made his way out of the convenience store.

"It's on the house, Detective," the clerk yelled, a

big grin on his seventeen-year-old face. He raised his fist in the air and made circles. "Go get 'em, man."

Anthony's mind raced. *If Hanif has touched her, even just touched her, I'll*—His radio interrupted his thoughts.

"Anthony, it's Grace. I'm on my way. ETA three minutes."

"Copy that. If you get there before me, go in. Don't knock, just go in. I'll be right behind you."

"Copy. Over."

Anthony's hands were slick with cold sweat. Only four blocks away he ran lights and sirens through holiday beach traffic and skidded up to the front door of Renee's building. He jumped out of his car, flashed his badge to the guard, who immediately let him in, and impatiently jabbed at the elevator buttons.

"Come on, come on," he muttered, frustrated at the slow moving machinery.

He looked over at the doorway to the stairs and weighed the option of running up ten flights, when the door dinged open. Once on the tenth floor, he sprinted to her door and barged in, hand on the handle of his weapon.

"Renee? Liz? Hanif?" There was no answer, no sound except for Beans, who had been put out on the patio. She barked excitedly, her paws pressed against the sliding-glass doors.

At that moment Grace charged in and stopped with a skid on the rug. "Nobody here?"

"Nobody here. I'm supposed to get a message. No, wait, hear a message."

"Tape recorder? Phone message?"

Grace headed toward Renee's room. Anthony headed toward the guest room.

"In here," Grace yelled. "There's an answering machine on the phone." She pressed the play button. A male voice came on, sounding sad, tired, and a little tinny on the mini-tape. There were long pauses between sentences.

"Liz. Liz, this is Steve. Really. I'm not dead. I'm not hurt or kidnapped or anything. I'm here. I need to talk with you. Please meet me at our bench under the flower arch in the park at noon today. I can explain it all, I swear. I'm—I'm so sorry about all this."

Anthony looked down at his watch. It was almost noon.

"Well, I'll be darned." Grace sat heavily down on the bed. "Liz's Steve? Alive? That kicks my theory all to hell."

"If he's the one extorting money from Liz, the women may be in trouble," Anthony said. "Where do you suppose this bench is?"

"He's probably talking about the flower arch at the Riverfront Park. Lots of lovers go there."

"Come on, we'll take my car." Anthony headed toward the door. "How do you know this stuff? The lots of lovers stuff?"

"Unlike you, I have a social life. And like hell you're driving. We'll take my car or go in separate vehicles."

"Slicky, you kill me. Come on, let's take the stairs."

Chapter 33

A Short Angry Ride

Riverfront Park was only a few miles from Renee's condo, on the river side of Ocean Drive.

During the short ride, Liz flipped from anger to relief, to disbelief, and then back to anger. "I'm going to kill him myself," she said through clenched teeth. "That son of a bitch was trying to scam his insurance money out of me." She made a fist and banged the side of the door.

Renee winced but wisely kept quiet.

"Sorry," Liz said, gingerly rubbing the door with her fingers.

It only took five minutes to reach the main entrance to the park, but the parking facility was several blocks farther.

The flower arch they sought stood smack in the middle.

"This is the closest point to the bench." Renee braked hard and pulled sharply over near some tall hedges covered in blood-red bougainvillea. "You hop out here. I'll go park and I'll be right behind you."

As soon as Liz could unbuckle her seatbelt, she jumped out and sprinted across the grass. Renee pulled quickly back out into traffic.

****

"There's the car," Dirt said, his voice at an excited pitch. He pointed through the windshield. "I thought we lost her at the turn by the big bushes."

"You can stop pointing, moron, I see her." Dante wheeled his car directly behind the red sedan and followed it into the parking garage.

Chapter 34

Collateral Damage

"Renee?"

The voice came from behind her as she beeped her car locked. She slowly turned around and saw two men approaching her too quickly for her liking. Her initial thought was that they wanted her purse, but she didn't have one, and besides they knew her name.

"Yes?" she said tentatively.

"Where's Liz?"

Seemed like an odd question. Renee didn't like these guys one bit. They were dirty, raggedy, and looked like every criminal she'd ever seen in court. Certainly not buddies of Liz.

"And you are?"

"Friends." The meaner-looking of the two tried a smile. It was scary, really more like a grimace. Adrenaline surged, making a cold spot in Renee's heart. Unsure of what to say or do next, she started to step back to her car.

"Not so fast, sweetie. I'm gonna' ask you again, but I'm not a patient man. Where's Liz?"

Renee tried to remember anything, any little bit of info, from her self defense class, but her mind remained annoyingly blank.

"Stay away from me or I'll scream," she said, her voice starting off strong, but cracking at the end. It wasn't until he pulled out a gun that her knees began to wobble.

"We don't need no screaming or someone is gonna' get hurt," the mean-looking one said. The two men had moved until they were on either side of her and had begun propelling her forward. "Now just walk with us and show us where Liz went. Nice and easy like, okay?"

The threesome tottered out of the shade of the garage and into the bright sunshine. Renee's face felt hot, her hands were cold, and her movements were stiff and unnatural. They walked past smiling, laughing couples, people listening to radios and sunning themselves on blankets piled high with coolers and Frisbees. How was it possible to just move easily through these people and have no one see that something was very wrong?

It only took a few minutes to reach the flower arch. It was on a little hill overlooking the river. As they neared, Renee could see Liz facing Steve. Renee squinted in the sun. Yep, it was Steve all right. Liz stood rigid, her head held high. Steve's mouth began moving. Then Liz hauled off and hit him across the face. The slap came from Georgia. At the sound, people nearby stared for a moment and then turned away, letting the couple have their privacy in the middle of a crowded place. Steve's hand flew to his face and his cheek began to redden.

"Well, look what we have here," the mean male said when they were still about ten feet away. "Steve, old boy, the last I saw you, you was bobbin' up and down in the water."

Steve slowly turned away from Liz and took a defensive stance. "Dante," Steve said, his voice angry, his mouth twisted in a snarl. He clenched his fists and took a menacing step forward. Dante stopped him by pulling up his shirt and showing him the gun stuck in his waistband. Then, he roughly tightened his grip on Renee's arm, making her stand on tiptoes for a moment.

"That gun doesn't scare me," Steve said, the contempt in his voice barely concealing his anger. "You're a lousy shot."

"Well, I'm scared of the gun," Renee said irritably. "Hello?"

"What's going on," Liz demanded, stepping up beside Steve. "What gun? Who are these guys?" Liz scowled at the way Dante was bruising her friend's arm. "Let her go."

"Now, no hard feelings, dude," Dante said, leveling a hard gaze at Steve. "It was just a job gone wrong is all. You were just—what do you call that? Oh yeah, collateral damage."

Liz's anger at Steve seemed momentarily forgotten. She lowered her voice. "Do you know these guys, Steve?"

"They tried to kill me, Liz." Steve's voice came out even and low, seemingly aware they were in public. "Last year at the fishing tournament. They took me miles out, shot at me, and threw me overboard."

Dirt snorted. "I told ya'. I said he wasn't dead." Dante's face darkened and his nostrils momentarily flared. Dirt jerked back as though physically struck, and finished lamely, "Well, I did."

Renee looked around helplessly. No one was paying any attention to the drama that was unfolding. She thought about screaming, but quickly stifled the urge when she saw little kids being pulled in a wagon on the sidewalk not six feet away. If Dante started shooting, someone was going to get hurt.

"I'm going to pound you into the seawall," Steve promised, ignoring Dirt, apparently assessing that he wasn't much of a threat. Steve returned Dante's menacing glare with his own black look. "You ruined my life. It was a year before I gained back my memory, found out who I was."

"Wait, wait. These guys shot at you?" Liz ran a hand through her hair. "Why?" Then she whirled around and pinned Steve with a withering look. "Are you trying to tell us you had amnesia?"

"Liz," Renee pleaded through clenched teeth. She nodded her head sideways at Dante. "Concentrate on the real issue at hand here."

"No, wait. This is a good one." Liz held up one hand putting everyone and everything on hold. "Amnesia for cripe's sake? I want to hear this." Liz crossed her arms tightly over her chest.

"Yeah, lover boy, tell us your big story," Dante said. "I'm gettin' a kick out of it myself."

Steve jabbed a finger at Dante and Dirt. "After they threw me overboard, I floated around for days. I don't even know how long I was out there. When I got picked up by some Russian freighter, I was pretty beat up."

"What's the matter? You don't like vodka?" Dante asked. The smirk on his face couldn't mask the tension underneath. "Stop your bitchin.' You're still alive, ain't ya'?"

Steve's hands had been by his side, but now he raised them and began massaging his knuckles. A tic made his cheek jump. His anger was palpable. When he took a reckless step forward, Liz grabbed his arm and held him back.

She stepped between the two men and faced Steve. "You were my fiancé, my future. You meant everything to me. When you disappeared, I wanted to die."

Dante rolled his eyes. "Aw, ain't this sweet."

"They really tried to kill you? But why?"

"They thought I was someone else," Steve said. "When they realized they had the wrong person, they tried to get rid of me."

Dirt had been standing in the background, standing in Dante's shadow. "It was that stupid Monica," he blurted out. "She told us the name of the boat we was supposed to hi-jack, but she got it wrong."

"Shut the hell up," Dante warned.

"Well, she did," Dirt whined. "Bitch was always stoned."

"Monica?" Liz and Steve said together.

"I should have known," Steve moaned.

"I ain't warnin' you again, Dirt," Dante warned, his voice low and menacing. "You want to be next overboard?"

Renee frantically looked around for help. Didn't anyone see this? How stupid was everyone?

"I worked that freighter, not knowing who I was or where I belonged," Steve continued, his voice thick. "I worked it until I thought I'd never get the stink out of my nose."

Steve took Liz's hands in his and gentled his tone. "Most ports we hit were hell holes, but when we pulled into Costa Rica, I knew I had found paradise. I left the ship, found work. I made a home in Tres Palmas. I started to live again." He closed his eyes and bowed his head. "I fell in love with a woman there, Liz."

Renee saw Liz stiffen at his words, but she didn't pull away, so he continued.

"We sold fruit at the open market. One day a kid went by with a loud boom box. I smiled and said to Corina, 'That's Liz's and my song.' All of a sudden, my life came rushing back. It hit me so hard it knocked me back against the wall and stole my breath. I didn't know what to do. My life with you. My life with her." Steve had tears in his eyes. "Liz, she's pregnant. I love her. I can't abandon her."

"You dumbass," Dante said.

"So what are you doing here?" Liz shot at him,

but more gently than before. "Why didn't you just stay dead?"

"I came back to tell you what happened. You deserved to know. And to sell my boat and condo so I could provide a better life for Corina and the baby. But when I got back here, Monica told me you had sold all my stuff and all the money was gone."

Liz's eyebrows lifted. "She did, did she?"

"I don't blame you," he added hastily. "You thought I was dead. We had gotten our wills done before the wedding. I had left everything to you anyway."

"But why did you even bother to find Monica? I don't understand."

"I saw her at the pier by accident. She said the only thing left was the life insurance money and that the check had just been issued. She said you'd never give it up if you knew I was still alive, so she came up with some scheme. I didn't even know exactly what the plan was, some e-mail thing or something. I admit I didn't want to know." An embarrassed red crept up his neck. "There was no honor on my part, no integrity in any of this. I have no excuse."

"Wait a minute, wait a minute," Dante interrupted angrily. "Monica was going to give you money?"

"Monica was supposed to pick up the money at the pier that night then bring it to the Coconut Palms Resort. I waited out back at their dock. We were going to split the money and both leave town."

"I tole ya' to stay away from Monica," Dirt said. He made a throaty noise and spit in the grass. "Ain't no job gone right with her yet."

"I'll take care of her when I see her, I promise you that, Dirt," Dante said. A vein pulsed in his forehead.

"If you're here to finish the job, it's between you and me," Steve said to Dante. Steve clenched his jaw and turned his full attention on Dante. He pulled Liz behind him and took a stance, leaving no mistake of his intentions. "I was a coward before, but not now. Leave the women out of it."

"Calm down, cowboy. For once Dirt's right, I left a loose end."

Dirt perked up and put a silly grin on his face.

Dante continued, "So you and I will settle our differences later, make no mistake about that. But right now, we need to take care of business here."

"And just what is your business here if you're not here for Steve?" Liz asked.

"My business is with you, darlin'," Dante said, jutting his chin at Liz.

"Me?" Liz scrunched up her nose in disgust. "I have no business with you."

"No business, huh?" Dante raised his eyebrows and made a palms-up gesture with his free hand. "Well, imagine my disappointment when I opened that little black case."

Liz appeared to see the dawn. "Oh, that business. So you were in cahoots with Monica, too. And she brought the money to you instead of Steve."

Pieces were rapidly clicking into place in Renee's mind. "The bag lady at the pier," Renee said.

Liz slapped the palm of her hand on her forehead. "Her shoe. The strap on her shoe. I watched that bag lady walk off the pier. I knew it seemed familiar, but I couldn't place it." Liz took a step toward Dante. "Where is she? I'll rip her face off."

"Never mind her. We want the money and we want it fast and I'm gonna hold your friend here," he shook Renee by the arm, making her wince, "until I get it."

"Now I don't understand," Steve said. "If Monica has the money, why are they here?"

"I didn't pay the ransom," Liz said. "The case

was filled with phony bills."

"I'm getting tired of you hurting my arm," Renee said irritably, pulling hard against Dante's grip. "Let me go."

"Yes, good idea. Let her go," a male voice yelled from the right side of Liz and Steve.

Everyone turned in that direction. Detective Graciano had his weapon drawn with a bead on Dante's heart. Renee was never so glad to see a lousy tie in all her life, even if it was on a ratfink, two-timing, no-account male.

"Anthony," Renee cried out, her voice betraying her bravado of a moment ago.

"I don't think so, not just yet," Dante said.

He released the grip he had on her just long enough to wrap his arm around her body and pull her in front of him as a shield. He produced the weapon from his waistband with his other hand and placed the barrel on the side of Renee's head. The click of the cocking mechanism was loud in her ear, a small sound that filled her whole world. A faint grunt came out of Renee, part misery, part disbelief.

Then Dante started dragging her backward.

Chapter 35

A Hot and Sizzling Day

When Anthony pulled his weapon, the nearby people in the park began scrambling and screaming. The women clutched their children tightly and the men alternated between their women's pleas to leave and their sense of being witness to imminent adventure.

Anthony held steady, but dared not fire with Renee in the way and a park full of people. He had been trained for situations like this, and he summoned up his inner strength to remain calm and assess the situation. He concentrated on the man holding Renee, the man called Dante, while remaining keenly aware of what was going on around him.

The man's partner, whose name he didn't catch, appeared almost dumbfounded by what had happened and reluctantly followed his friend, but at a distance. Anthony determined that that jerk wasn't a threat at this point, but experience told him to never trust him to be as dumb as he looked.

Anthony repeatedly ordered Dante to drop his weapon and release the woman. At each command, his voice became harsher and his desire to take this guy down grew stronger. Anthony kept pace with the pair. Each tense step Dante took backward, Anthony moved forward.

"Your time is running out. Drop your weapon and get on the ground. Now."

"Nah, I'm happy. I got lots of time. Don't much like the ground," Dante retorted.

"This won't end good for you," Anthony all but growled, "you know there's more cops on the way. Do yourself a favor and end it here with me."

Dante tightened his grip on Renee, making her yell out. Her cries were like ice picks to Anthony's heart. His anger was now white hot, threatening to override his cop's instincts. He wanted to hurl himself at Dante. He itched to feel his fists smash his ugly face.

"You hurt her and by the time I'm done with you, your mama won't even recognize you," Anthony said through clenched teeth. He shortened the distance between himself and Dante.

"You got something for this woman?" Dante let out a loud snort. "My good luck. Makes her more valuable." Dante dropped his head and gave Anthony a half-lidded stare. "She stays with me. You get any closer and I'll hurt her. Hurt her bad. You hear me?"

****

It was such a surreal moment that Renee had lost her ability to reason. She watched the scene unfolding around her as though she weren't in it. People were scattering around her in slow motion. Anthony shouted at Dante, and Dante kept moving backward.

For the first time in Renee's life, her mortality was no longer a conjecture. It was close and coldly beckoning, teasing her, whispering in her ear. If that wasn't enough to terrify her, there was the realization that this could also end badly for Liz and Anthony.

She desperately tried to put together a plan. She never thought of herself as a helpless victim, always figured she'd be cool under fire, but here she was, inching backward in a crazy man's grip, and she had no idea what to do. It was ironic that she was surrounded all day at work by criminals and low-life characters, and yet when something bad happened to her, it happened out here in the sunshine, with kites flying and the sounds of water craft in the background.

She had to get a grip. She focused on Anthony to see if he was directing her to do something. He wasn't. Steve was right behind the detective, but he wasn't looking at her either.

She saw Liz waving her arms and yelling something. Renee struggled to pick Liz's voice out of the riot of sounds.

"Sweat, Renee," Liz screamed through cupped hands. "Sweat. Sweat."

Sweat? Baffled, Renee vehemently shook her head no. "What? I don't understand. What are you saying?"

Then a calm washed over her that felt almost physical. Renee's eyes opened wide in understanding. SWET. Shins, weight, eyes, and testicles, from her self defense class where the women were taught how to fight back.

Since her back was to Dante, the eyes and testicles were out. Shins? Maybe. But she could definitely use her weight.

She mouthed "weight" to Liz, who immediately sprinted over to where Anthony held his stance and yelled in his ear. Anthony looked over at Renee, hesitated a moment, glanced past her for a fraction of a second, then locked his eyes on hers and nodded his approval. Renee immediately let herself slump down in a dead weight as though she had fainted.

Dante, caught by surprise, made a grab with both his arms in a desperate attempt to keep a grip on her. As Renee slid out of his grasp and scrambled away, she heard a sizzling sound. Dante let out a primal scream, stiffened, and dropped to the ground where Detective Slikowski stood over him with a hot stun gun.

Chapter 36

Getting His Yellow Ducks...

It took over two hours to process the three men. Anthony divided his time between the booking procedures and doing the interviews in the Detective Bureau. Steve and Dirt shuffled meekly from work station to work station completing the different portions, apparently resigned to their fates, but Dante raised bloody hell and had to be placed in a security cell. His mug shot showed a very angry, disheveled male, a large red welt on his neck. He glared into the lens, being held firmly upright by two huge JPD officers.

In the west wing, where it was air conditioned and pleasantly furnished in calming colors, Anthony finished up his interview with Liz Sutton. Under his guidance, she had given a very detailed accounting. When she finished, Anthony hit the print button and slid the statement to her across the table.

"If that statement is true, and you have no corrections, additions or deletions, then please write your name on both pages where it's indicated."

Liz signed her statement and pushed it back to Anthony. Her tightly folded arms and frosty manner should have been a warning of the storm to come. Not expecting any problems, Anthony took the documents and started to countersign and date on his spots. He found he could barely write under her glare.

"What?"

"I have no intention of going out with you," she said, her lips tight, her eyes flashing a warning no man could possibly miss.

Anthony's eyebrows came together, and he looked up from the paperwork. He had to admit, he hadn't seen that coming.

"Okaaay," he said gently. "But I don't remember asking, actually."

"Don't be cute," she snapped.

Anthony studied the initials scratched in the table, trying to stall. Was he so out of the loop with women that he didn't even know what was going on any more? First Renee had run him up and down the street, and now Liz was taking a turn. He seemed to be stuck in stupid.

"I'm not following," he said honestly. Rejection was every guy's nightmare, but Anthony was getting turned down by a woman he hadn't even asked out. A new low; even for him.

"You know Renee likes you."

Snapshots of his grammar school playground flickered through his head. His best buddy running up and handing him a note from the red-headed girl with the pony tail. DO YOU LIKE ME? written in shaky block letters. Two little squares on the bottom. CHECK HERE. One for yes, one for no.

"And I like her, too," he said slowly, mentally checking the yes box.

"Then how could you treat her so badly then?" The sharp bite of her tone felt like a slap.

Anthony held up a hand in a stopping motion. "Wait, wait, wait. What are you talking about?"

"Leading her on," she said through clenched teeth. "Kissing her while secretly wanting to ask me out."

"I didn't lead her on. I did kiss her." A warm,

pleasant bump touched his heart at the memory, then abruptly drained as he realized what Liz had said. His head snapped up. "Secretly what?"

"Don't try to deny it, mister. Grace told us everything."

Anthony sat in perfect silence for a moment. "Grace told you," he finally said.

"She sure did. And it about broke Renee's heart." Liz had lowered her voice, but it was still tight with emotion. "Do you know how fragile she is? Do you even care?"

"Grace told you?"

"What, are you deaf, too? Yes, Grace told us that when this case is finished you were dying to ask me out."

Anthony slumped back in his chair and let out a small groan. "Grace," he said softly. Of all of his boneheaded ideas, telling Grace that lie was the boniest.

He looked over at the fireball that was Renee's best friend. He had to admire her loyalty. Leaning forward, he took both of Liz's hands firmly in his and told her in detail what an idiot he was. By the time he had finished, Liz's eyes were moist, and she had put on a little smile.

They left the interview room, and he settled her in the reception area. "You can wait here for Renee. She has to finish her statement and I have to read Grace the riot act." He dug in his pockets and found some change. Dropping coins in the vending machine, he said, "Here, have a terrible coffee."

"You're going to straighten this all out with Renee tonight, right?"

Anthony faced her. "Liz, when I look at her sometimes I forget to breathe."

He could tell Liz liked his answer, because she relaxed, but strain still tightened her face.

"I'm worried about her, Anthony."

"I know you are. You're a good friend."

"After her divorce there were parts of her she managed to fill again, pieces of herself she worked back into place. But I don't know if she's ready for a relationship."

"I won't hurt her, Liz," Anthony vowed. "And I won't rush her."

Liz put a hand on his arm and gave it a little squeeze. "You feel like a promise. I'm going to let myself believe it's possible." Turning him toward to the door, she gave him a little push. "Go on then."

****

Now it all made sense—the slamming of doors, flinging of roses, frost in the air. Thankfully, Renee wasn't a crazy woman whose moods changed by the hour. She had good reason to despise him.

The door to interview room #2, where Grace was finishing up with Ms. Rose, was cracked open. Anthony gave a curt rap on the glass with his knuckles and indicated with a jerk of his head that Grace should join him in the hallway.

"You almost done in there?" he asked when the door clicked shut behind her.

"Just wrapping it up. No surprises. How about you?"

Anthony gave her a hard stare. "Yeah, I got one surprise. What the hell did you do?"

Grace gave him a quizzical look. "Huh?"

"You told Liz Sutton that I wanted to date her?"

Grace cringed back against the tile wall and folded her arms over her chest. "Oh, crap."

Anthony jammed his hands in his pockets and paced back and forth. "You are always on me about finding a woman, and I just wanted a little peace, so I lied to you."

"What do you mean you lied? You don't want to go out with Liz Sutton?"

"No, Grace, I don't." He stopped pacing and

234

whirled on her. "And I sure as hell didn't think you'd go tell her." His voice was steely cool. "Isn't that against some kind of police procedure?" He jabbed a finger at her. "Yes, yes, it is. There's some sort of statute or something."

Grace rolled her eyes. "You're pitiful." For a moment she looked like she might be feeling what would pass for guilt then she shook it off and squared her shoulders. "It all boils down to the fact that you shouldn't have opened your mouth." She poked a finger into his chest. "This is entirely your fault, and you can just go back in there and fix it with Liz."

"You're not getting the full picture. I'm not interested in Liz." Anthony hesitated a moment, then plunged on. "But I am crazy about Renee." He could feel a warm spot starting to form on his cheeks, just above his dimples. Certain he was turning red, he shoved frustrated hands in his pockets and jutted his chin out. "So there. You happy, woman?"

"Ohhh," Grace said. She stood in the hallway studying him, not unlike a specimen in a jar, until he was squirmy and uncomfortable. "Are you sure you're not mixing up your misplaced sense of saving everyone for the fact that you've got heat for this woman?"

He was besotted, he ruefully admitted it. What started out as an innocent physical attraction and amusing infatuation had quickly grown wings.

"I think of her every second of the day." He shook his head. "That's not normal, is it?"

Grace broke out into a huge grin. "As long as it doesn't get you shot on the job. What are you going to do about it?"

"I straightened it out with Liz. Now, I'm going to go in there and tell Renee." He jerked his head at Grace. "And you're going in there with me."

"Okay."

He studied her suspiciously. "You agreed awfully quick."

"Honey, I wouldn't miss this for the world," Grace grabbed him by his purple tie, the one with the yellow ducks on it, and tugged him toward the interview room door. A scowl crossed her face at the material scrunched in her hand.

"Tell me this was a gag gift. Please."

Chapter 37

... In A Row

In the end, Anthony decided to go into Renee's room by himself, but he hesitated at the threshold.

"You might want to turn away," he said to Grace. "I'm about to struggle."

"And she might hurt you," Grace added. "Is your life insurance current?"

"Ha-ha."

"I'll foam the runway in case you go down in flames." Grace put a hand on his back. "Go on, get it over with." She propelled him into the room and gently shut the door.

When he first entered and sat, he was positioned across the table. It seemed too far away for a personal conversation, so he moved. When he switched to the seat next to her, he noted that Renee inched her chair away, but she didn't bolt. The air in the little room was practically glacial and her face unmistakably said *don't mess with me*. Anthony blew on his hands, giving himself a minute to compose.

"All right, here goes. I'm not in here to talk about the case," he said, looking earnestly into her face. She remained silent. If she was curious, he couldn't tell. One thing that was crystal clear was her disapproval. It read like a newspaper headline. He faltered, wishing he had had the time to prepare better. Thoughts came into his head in a disorderly, undecipherable way. He wiped his palms on his pants. Man, he couldn't afford to blow this. This woman, who sat rigid and pale by his side, was going to be the love of his life. He knew that as sure as he knew the moon was going to pull the tide back out in the morning.

A shadow at the door window interrupted his thought process, such as it was. Anthony jerked his head in a "get-lost" motion, and Grace slid out of view. Renee appeared to be getting antsy. The room was cramped, and it smelled rather unpleasantly of past occupants. He cleared his throat.

"I know Grace told you and Liz that I was talking about dating Liz after this case is over."

"I don't give a rat's ass what you do," she said, her words like marbles dropping in a glass jar. "But know this, Liz will never go out with you."

"Fair enough," he said, "Except that I lied to Grace."

Studying her to see if that disclosure would have a reaction, he was given nothing but a cool, stone wall to bang his head against. He ran a hand through his hair.

"Look, Grace is my best friend."

"So what?" she said, biting off the words and spitting them out.

"She cares about me, but she also drives me crazy."

"And I care about this why?"

"If I told her I liked German Sheppards, she'd be buying me one for Christmas. I'd get ties with dogs on them."

Renee looked sharply at his tie. "Couldn't hurt."

He let that go. "So what I'm saying is she goes overboard. She gets involved where she shouldn't. She messes in my life."

"Good for you. Are we done here, Detective? It's

getting late."

It was time to get to the point.

"I knew Grace would never leave me alone if I told her I was attracted to—a woman," he finished lamely. The room suddenly seemed twice as small as he remembered. "She would never condone me dating someone whose case I was working on. I wanted her off my back, so I lied to her. I told her I wanted to date Liz."

"You are so pathetic."

"Yeah, well, see I knew she would leave me alone for awhile. I never expected her to blurt that out to you and Liz."

"Why are you telling me? Shouldn't you be telling Liz?"

Afraid her wall was so painfully constructed that he might not be able to climb over, his logic was to ease her down off it. "Then after the case I'd be free to date whoever I wanted." He nodded encouragingly at her. "You see?"

"No. Is this supposed to make me feel better or something? Because it's not."

There was hurt, anger, and maybe a little confusion in her eyes.

"Renee, I lied to Grace. I didn't want to date Liz, I wanted to date you." There, he finally exposed his heart. Would she stomp it to bits now? "Want to date you," he quickly amended.

She sat quietly for a moment. When she bit her lower lip, it made him dizzy. "Me?" she said in a voice that sounded strangely husky.

"Yes. Can't you tell I'm crazy about you?"

She turned to face him head on and let her arms fall in her lap. "People that you're crazy about, do you always yell at them and order them around?" Anthony could see her defenses slip a little.

"Like a drill sergeant."

"I see."

He thought he detected the start of a smile, though it still appeared broken in spots. Encouraged, he reached over and gently took her hands. They were so small and cold. He began to warm them between his own. She didn't pull away.

"And do you stomp around and generally act like a maniac?" she continued.

"That's just me worried to death about you. I didn't trust Hanif."

"Some detective. Hanif is just an exchange student," she said, but her voice was lighter, teasing.

"I know, I know." He shook his head. "I can't think straight when I'm around you."

"You were worried about me?" A smile played with the corners of her mouth.

"Renee, I was mad about you the moment I saw you. That day when you fell on me, I wanted to stay like that forever."

"You did?" Her cheeks were starting to come alive with color. "It wasn't all that bad for me either," she said in a small voice.

Anthony couldn't keep his grin from showing. Although he had fought it, he had known that very day that this was the woman he had been waiting for. He inched nearer to her chair. If he leaned just six inches, he could lick her neck. That thought made him crazy.

"You know I was married before," she said.

"Yes." He was afraid to go there.

"And you know it ended badly."

He knew because he had snooped around but he didn't want to tell her that. "I heard something," he said vaguely.

"My divorce was ugly and very public. It played out right in my own backyard, in front of everyone I worked with. All our friends were cops, so I had to see them at trials or depositions."

Anthony nodded, picturing her going it alone

while her ex cavorted with all his buds. It made him angry. He reached over and brushed his thumb gently across her cheek. "You want me to shoot him?" he said, mostly kidding.

That finally made her smile and that act alone lifted his heart. He made a mental note to himself to always make her laugh.

"Appreciate the offer but no."

Anthony pulled her closer to him. He lowered his head so that his mouth was spectacularly close to hers. "It's okay, go on."

"It became almost impossible for me to go through a normal day, but over time, I worked through it. And I stayed away from cops. All cops."

"I understand." A flash of alarm swept through him. She wasn't going to blow him off? A light sweat began to form on his temples.

"I have tragic taste in men."

"I know you're scared, and I've done some things wrong, but I know I can make them right." He tried to keep the pleading out of his voice.

"When I first met you, you looked and smelled like trouble, or at the very least an adventure. And I hadn't had one in a very long time."

He grinned. "Yeah?"

"I was immediately drawn to you and that scared me."

"Scared of getting involved?"

"That, yes. And of you smothering me. You're awfully bossy, you know."

"Yeah, I gotta work on that."

"Or worse, you not needing me once the novelty fades."

Anxious to seal the deal, Anthony raised her chin and captured her eyes with his own. He was relieved to see they mirrored his desire. Mere inches separated them. He would be a fool to let this moment pass. He leaned down and brushed her lips, lightly at first then stronger as his passion quickly took hold. She melted into him, meeting his kisses with her own, matching his urgency. The scent of her skin and hair was intoxicating. He pulled her closer needing the length of her against him. When he felt her tremble he began to pull away, but she put her hand on the back of his neck and drew him down again. He reveled in the tenderness of her caress, marveled how their very souls intertwined through their breath. Her body movements hinted of things to come if he was a very good boy. He never wanted a woman so badly. A small groan escaped his mouth when they parted. He was a drowning man and he didn't care.

"Now look what you've done," he whispered in her ear. "Every time I smell a sweaty interview room, I'm going to get aroused."

A noise in the hallway abruptly brought them back to the present. They scooted their chairs apart. She tucked her blouse in and fluffed her hair with her fingers. He adjusted his tie and worked a knot out of his shoulders.

"Why don't we do this," he suggested. "Why don't we take this real, real slow and give ourselves a chance to get used to the idea."

"You'll work on not ordering me around?"

"Yes, absolutely. And you'll work on letting someone in your life again?"

"Tall order."

"Not an order," he said gently. "A request."

She appeared to be mulling it over then lasered him, a direct hit from under half closed lashes. "Can I pick out your ties?"

Chapter 38

A Feel-good Spot

Two months later...

Renee and Liz sat on the hard metal benches at the San Jose Airport in Costa Rica, waiting for their flight to be called. All around them, sunburned tourists sipped iced juice drinks and rechecked their boarding passes.

"Boy," Renee said, "I know I was only involved on the sidelines in all this drama, but I have to say that felt really good, didn't it?" She took off her floppy straw hat and fanned herself. "You think the air is working in this place?"

Liz sat slumped over her carry-on case, fiddling with the zipper. She absent-mindedly rubbed a spot above her heart.

"I still feel that warmth and it's been three days, too."

"That's a feel-good spot," Renee said. "If we're lucky, maybe it'll never go away."

Liz nodded. "That would be all right." She sat back and studied the people bustling around. "Thanks for coming with me."

Renee grinned. "Anytime you want to search out your dead fiancé's pregnant wife and give her the hundred thousand dollars you got for selling Steve's boat and practically make her faint, you just call me,

I'm in."

"I'm pretty sure it's a one-time thing."

"Yeah, probably is."

The two friends sat in comfortable silence.

"It's so pretty here," Renee said. "I can understand why he wanted to stay."

The water in the bay had been achingly blue, fringed with green palms and lush vegetation. It had almost hurt their eyes to look at it. Small, yellow fishing boats, the color designating the Tres Palmas fleet, dotted the waters like flower petals in a pool. There were no docks, no cruise ships in the harbor. The land held no wires, no cables. Flowers rioted around doorframes and tumbled out of window boxes.

Each morning on the open terrace at the hotel, much to the women's delight, little green birds with bright red markings would swoop down and snatch pieces of toast off their plates, then perch above them on shady limbs to eat their stolen breakfast.

"As pretty as a damn post card," Liz said. "Except maybe for that old, rusted cab we had to take to Corina's place."

"Hanif would absolutely love it here."

"How is Hanif doing?" Liz asked, becoming momentarily cross-eyed trying to peel a tiny strip of sunburned skin from her nose. "Did you get his charge dropped down to a civil fine like you wanted?"

"Yes, he's back on the right side of the law. And Mom says, he's off the charts in school."

Liz sat back and stared at the ceiling lights. "Corina's a pretty thing, isn't she?" she said softly.

"She is, but we both know Steve has exquisite taste in women."

"And very pregnant."

"And very pregnant. You handled this whole thing very well, Liz. I'm proud of you."

"Well, the insurance company was sure happy

when I returned that money." She studied her friend a moment then added, "Maybe I should have kept it."

Renee knew she wasn't serious.

"You and I could be on the beach in Tahiti with gorgeous beach boys serving us tropical drinks with little straw umbrellas."

"Yeah, well," Renee dismissed the idea with a backward wave of her hand. "I hear Tahiti isn't all it's cracked up to be."

"Really? Well, I guess it all worked out then."

Renee nodded in agreement. "Except maybe for Steve."

"Yes, well, Steve." Liz shrugged her shoulders. "I can't help him anymore. I told him I'd write and keep his commissary account full, but..." her voice drifted off.

Renee gave her a moment to compose. When Liz continued, her voice grew stronger. "With good behavior, he'll only do three years. At that point, he can decide what to do with his condo. I'll keep it rented for him until then. He'll be fine when he gets out."

"Is there any chance—" Renee started.

"No chance in the world," Liz broke in. "Too much time has passed. Too much has happened."

Renee put a comforting arm around her friend.

"And he has a son coming," Liz added.

Neither of them spoke. Their friendship spoke volumes.

"Did I tell you what Sonja told me about Dante and Dirt?" Renee asked.

"No, what'd she say?"

"The Dante guy entered a plea of not guilty. He said he was just in the park getting some sun or something, and he got jumped on by the police. He's actually talking about suing for police brutality.

"Now Dirt, on the other hand, sang like he was

auditioning for *American Idol*. He's trying to cut a deal to turn state's evidence against Dante."

"Well, for being the dumb one, that's pretty smart."

"I guess. Unless Dante gets hold of him. How about Monica? Anything on her?"

"Nope. She's like the wind, as they say. I hope she never comes back, frankly." Liz shifted her position. "Could they make these seats any harder?"

Renee glanced at her watch. It was almost time to start boarding.

"Is Anthony picking us up in Miami," Liz asked.

Renee warmed at the mention of his name. "Yes, and he's taking me out for dinner tonight at the Green Parrot."

"Ooh, that's a nice place," Liz said. She looked into Renee's eyes. "He put a sparkle there that I haven't seen for a long time. Now, there's something that worked out."

"And that feels good, too." Renee bit her lower lip. "Imagine me going with a cop?" A little flutter bumped her heart at the thought of her newfound love. Things were definitely going well in the romance department.

"Know what he did last week?" Renee said. "He left a white daisy on my pillow with all the petals plucked off except one."

"He loves me." Liz crinkled her nose in pleasure for her friend.

"Who knew a tough guy like that could be so damn sweet, huh?"

"Told you so," Liz said matter-of-factly, ducking from the mock punch that came her way.

Renee had finally taken that last step and opened her heart. Anthony was solid, stable and sincere. If he hurt her, it wouldn't be on purpose. They shared lighthearted days and soft, secret sounds in the night. He was better than a warm cookie.

There is an old Chinese proverb that says, "Do not regret going slow. Regret only standing still." If Renee could needlepoint, she would hang that in her living room. Afraid she was going to tear up, she pointed to a kiosk as a distraction. "Hey, we have enough time to go buy one more T-shirt."

Liz looked over to the splash of colorful shirts hanging on racks and dumped in disorganized piles all over the table. She stifled a groan. "No more for me. I think I have four now. Did you get one for Anthony?"

Renee rummaged around in a huge shopping bag between her legs and pulled out a purple T-shirt with yellow birds marching across the chest.

"It's perfect." Liz grinned.

A word about the author...

Originally a travel agent, Jody completely switched gears, returned to school, and became a court reporter. Now instead of traveling the world she works with murderers, rapists, and thieves, who are almost never in a good mood. Being assigned to the chief judge in Broward County, Florida, exposed her to a wide spectrum of cases; from funny to tragic to bizarre to downright creepy; she has reported everything from a homeless guy who jumped the turnstile on the Metrorail and is now in jail for not having a quarter, to the Tamiami Strangler, a serial killer who murdered six women.

Positive that in a past life she was a writer (or possibly a dancehall girl) Jody has always incorporated writing in her life. Now the stories she is exposed to in court, the mayhem, the heartbreak, and particularly the black humor, all make writing a breeze, and she almost never falls asleep at the keyboard anymore.

On a personal note, Jody is an only child who had an only child (claiming she didn't breed well in captivity). Leaving the Florida heat behind, she now resides in a charming little town in New England.

Thank you for purchasing
this Wild Rose Press publication.
For other wonderful stories of romance,
please visit our on-line bookstore at
www.thewildrosepress.com.

For questions or more information
contact us at
info@thewildrosepress.com.

The Wild Rose Press
www.TheWildRosePress.com

To visit with authors of The Wild Rose Press
join our yahoo loop at
http://groups.yahoo.com/group/thewildrosepress/